Cat in Glass

Nancy Etchemendy

Cat in Glass

and
Other
Tales
of the
Unnatural

Cricket Books
Chicago

The Flat-Brimmed Hat—originally published in *Twilight Zone Magazine,* April 1987. **Clotaire's Balloon**—originally published in *The Magazine of Fantasy and Science Fiction,* November 1984. **The Lily and the Weaver's Heart**—originally published in *The Armless Maiden and Other Tales for Childhood's Survivors,* Terri Windling, ed., Tor Books, March 1995. **Cat in Glass**—originally published in *The Magazine of Fantasy and Science Fiction,* July 1989. **Lunch at Etienne's**—originally published in *The Magazine of Fantasy and Science Fiction,* November 1987. **The Sailor's Bargain**—originally published in *The Magazine of Fantasy and Science Fiction,* April 1989. **The Tuckahoe**—originally published in *Shadows 8,* Charles L. Grant, ed., Doubleday, 1985. **Shore Leave Blacks**—originally published in *The Magazine of Fantasy and Science Fiction,* March 1990.

Library of Congress Cataloging-in-Publication Data

Etchemendy, Nancy.
  Cat in glass and other tales of the unnatural / Nancy Etchemendy.—
1st ed.
      p. cm.
Contents: The flat-brimmed hat — Clotaire's balloon — The lily and the weaver's heart — Cat in glass — Lunch at Etienne's — The sailor's bargain — The Tuckahoe — Shore leave blacks.
  ISBN 0-8126-2674-5 (cloth : alk. paper)
  1. Young adult fiction, American. 2. Supernatural—Juvenile fiction.
[1. Short stories. 2. Supernatural—Fiction.] I. Title.
  PZ7.E84 Cat 2002
  [Fic]—dc21

                                                        2002008788

For Cecily

❖ ❖ ❖

O.K., there really was a witch in our closet.

Contents

Cat in Glass

THE FLAT-BRIMMED HAT

Balanced on the crumbly bedrock cliff at the edge of the old
V & T grade, Kathy wondered whether she really wanted to
do it, and if so, whether this was really the *way* she wanted
to do it. She took a deep breath, then another and another.
The jagged rocks and the green valley far below flickered
like an old-time movie. Dizzy, she backed up a step and
forced herself to breathe more evenly. If she was going to do
it, she wanted to do it on purpose—not just hyperventilate
herself into unconsciousness and drop over the edge like a
sack of potatoes.

The thin, sweet call of a mountain blue-
bird drifted down to her from a
nearby juniper.

The wild smells of sagebrush and piñon pine and sun-warmed rocks rode on the back of the wind that came up the grade. She really wanted to do it. There was, after all, more to life than bluebirds and sagebrush. She stepped forward, closed her eyes, ducked her head, and stuck her arms out in front of her. The whole business would be much easier if she pretended she was jumping off the high dive at the municipal swimming pool. One, two, three. She bent her knees, considered holding her nose, then realized she didn't need to. Not this time.

Someone grabbed her by the shoulder. A resonant contralto poured through the high desert stillness. "Hey, cookie. For crissakes. Give us both a break. You don't really want to do that."

Kathy went rigid, opened her eyes, and silently mouthed the words, Hell, hell, hell.

Perhaps she had made a mistake. Perhaps she hadn't walked four hours to get to this place. Perhaps this wasn't really the summit of a road so dilapidated that only hikers, horses, and lunatics in jeeps dared traverse it. No. She was incapable of that particular mistake. She had lived down there in the frigging valley all her life. She knew nobody came to this place. The old-timers had forgotten about it, and the newcomers didn't care about good views unless they could see them from a living room window.

There were chinks in Kathy's black despair. And anger, like blasting powder, was packed inside them all. She curled her hands into hard, rock fists and turned around.

A small woman stood before her, slender hands settled on slender hips. The woman regarded Kathy with sunlit brown eyes and an infuriating half smile. She wore an embroidered cotton shirt like the ones Kathy had often admired in the window of Parker's Saddle Shop. But the flat-brimmed hat that rode far back among her short glossy curls looked South American, and the cut of her high-waisted denims marked her as a city jerk.

Kathy put on the sneer she used whenever she had to deal with unpleasant people—her drunken stepfather, the landlady's bitchy daughter, and lately Reese Vanderberg as well.

"Who the hell are you? Why don't you just mind your own damn business?" Kathy spit the words out like lit firecrackers.

The woman grinned. She had strong, white teeth. A network of spider-web laugh lines appeared at the corners of her eyes. She held out her left hand. A jagged, pale scar ran from the first joint of her index finger to the second.

Kathy knew the scar. She had one exactly like it on her own left index finger. She blinked, struggling to remember whether she had actually jumped off the cliff. Maybe she was dreaming this on the way to the ground. Or maybe she was already dead.

"Just call me Kate," said the woman. "Whether you like it or not, my own damn business includes yours."

"Huh?" said Kathy, scratching her nose. It burned. She'd been out in the sun too long.

"Sweetie, you don't have to understand it. Just believe it. I'm you. I'm the woman you're going to be twenty years from now. Look at me. Why are you trying to screw me up like this?"

Kathy squinted. Now that she thought of it, the woman did look a little familiar, in a middle-aged kind of way.

Kate took a cellophane-wrapped cigar out of her pocket. She offered it to Kathy. "No thanks," said Kathy. "They make me sick."

"Yeah, they used to make me sick, too." Chuckling, Kate peeled away the cellophane. "Ten years from now, you'll buy a sports car and take up smoking just because you like the idea of a woman driving fast cars and smoking good cigars."

"Oh yeah?" said Kathy. She was beginning to feel the way she had years ago after she had drunk a bottle of vanilla with a friend—a little queasy and not altogether certain about the line between what was real and what was not.

Kate stuck the cigar in her mouth and sucked on it, unlit. She took Kathy firmly by the arm and led her away from the precipice, back onto the road.

"So what's bothering you this time? I can't quite remember," she said, her words wet and pleasant.

"If you were really me, you'd remember," said Kathy.

Kate laughed and nipped the end off the cigar with her large, familiar teeth. "Sweetie, you're so dramatic. I admit you don't come this close very often, but you think about it all the time. How the hell am I supposed to keep one trauma separate from the next?"

"I don't think about it all the time!" said Kathy.

Kate snorted as she lit a wooden match and cupped it expertly away from the breeze. "Give me a break," she said, puffing until a cloud of white smoke rose from between her hands.

Kathy kicked a pebble. She listened as it rattled down the precipice, striking other rocks on its way to the ground. She shivered. "I got jilted."

"Oh yeah," said Kate. "I remember now. That golden-haired jerk. Reese what's-his-name."

"Reese Vanderberg is not a jerk. And how would you know? You can't even get his name right."

"Look. I can't get his name right because twenty years from now, you won't be able to get his name right. Twenty years from now, Reese Vanderberg will be an insurance salesman with a Lincoln Continental and two preppy jerk kids, whom he will have gotten from that blond airhead, Sally what's-her-name. Believe me, cookie, there are better things than that in store for you."

Kathy kicked another pebble. "Sally, huh? Yeah. Sally's a creep. And if Reese would rather have Sally, then he's a creep, too."

"Come on. It's not that he'd rather have Sally. And it's not as if you're up here getting ready to jump off a cliff just because Vanderberg jilted you. You say that to me because it's what you'd say to some stranger. But we both know there's more to it than that."

Kathy had sat awake in a chair all night, swept and tumbled by the old familiar river of dark thoughts. Reese had tried to make love to her, just as all the others had, and she had tried to let him, just as she always did. But her body had betrayed her, in the pattern that had grown smooth through repetition—smooth as a stone in a glacial creek. She had stiffened, pulled back. She felt the surprise in his hands, saw it flutter like the shadow of a luna moth across his face. She grabbed her clothes and ran. And Reese shouted after her, "Bitch! Prick-teasing bitch!" Just like they all did.

She hunched her shoulders and looked over at Kate. Kate wore the dusty hat as if it were a part of her, tipped back in an easy way to reveal damp curls just beginning to turn gray around her ears. Her whole body told a story of pleasure, in the swing of her shoulders as she walked, in the rise and fall of her small breasts as she tasted the sweet tobacco smoke. The lines around Kate's eyes and mouth looked custom made to mysterious specifications. Those lines cradled smiles, frowns, and dreams the way Kathy had always wanted to cradle a man. She was beautiful.

A dull red flower of grief blossomed inside her. She could never be like that. Never. A tear splattered onto her boot. "Hell," said Kathy.

Kate shoved a handkerchief into Kathy's hand. Kathy scrubbed viciously at her eyes. The handkerchief was made of lavender silk and had a violet embroidered on it. It smelled like cigars. She wadded it into a wrinkled ball and flung it back at Kate. "Now I know you're not me," she said. "I wouldn't be caught dead carrying around a thing like that."

Kate stuck the handkerchief back in her pants pocket and gave Kathy a sidelong frown. She turned her gaze back to the rutted road and the junipers that clung to the hillside above it. "All right. You want to know why you're gonna be carrying silk handkerchiefs around someday? Because there's a man in your future who likes them."

Kathy shook her head. "There's no man in my future."

"Suit yourself," said Kate, shrugging.

Kathy wondered why she would want a man in her future anyway. She shoved her hands deep into the pockets of her wash-softened Levi's and found the arrowhead Reese had given her there. She rubbed her thumb hard along the sharp flint edge. She thought about the way her father had beaten her mother until she couldn't stand up anymore. She thought about her stepfather, who acted like a stud in rut every time he got drunk. Her heart kept telling her they weren't all like that. But her body just wouldn't believe it.

Kathy looked at Kate again. Kate smiled at her. Kate's face seemed so much at home with smiles. Was it true? Was it possible that Kathy's own face would someday look like that? In the desert sun, something sparkled on one of the fingers of Kate's left hand. A plain gold wedding ring. Kathy blinked, dazzled.

They had been walking as they talked, Kathy following the older woman down the rutted, white road, so preoccupied with her own pain that she paid no attention. Now they rounded a curve, and there, crouched like a steel tiger, sat a Jeep, almost brand-new, with all the extras, the kind Kathy had always wanted. A light coating of dust covered its deep burgundy paint. Kathy stared at it, dreaming of places a machine like that could take her, of hillsides and valleys and canyons a million miles away.

"Is that yours? Where'd you get it?"

Kate rubbed her neck slowly, gazing at the Jeep as if she herself found it somewhat mysterious. "Yeah. It's mine. I bought it about six months ago from a guy in Manhattan who told me it could take me places I'd never believe." She gave Kathy a little grin. "I guess he was right."

"Manhattan?" said Kathy.

"Yeah. Manhattan," said Kate, eyes sparkling. "Hop in."

Kathy climbed into the passenger seat, yelping as the heat from the sun-baked black Naugahyde crept through her thin shirt. Kate tossed her hat into the back, ran her fingers through her sweat-soaked hair. She winked.

"What do you think, sweetie? Isn't this better than some blond jerk's Lincoln Continental?"

Kathy grinned. "Could be," she said.

Kate caressed the gearshift lever and twisted the key in the ignition. "Put your seat belt on, cookie."

The Jeep roared and leaped off in a cloud of sand and thunder. Kathy clung to the seat the way she had clung to Reese when he took her on the double Ferris wheel at the county fair.

Kate drove like a maniac, laughing as they fishtailed around curves and sailed airborne over chuckholes and washouts. The cigar jutted from the corner of her mouth, alternately emitting vast windblown clouds and waving as Kate chewed on it.

At the top of the V & T grade, Kate shifted down, and the Jeep's fat tires screamed as they grabbed the pavement of the main road to Silver City, the nearly abandoned mining town on the other side of the hills. They roared like a fire engine past the crumbling graveyard and the entrance to the old Fairman Tunnel. They sprayed dust at the Sutro Hotel and startled the mangy brown dog that lay in the sun on Main Street. When they skidded to a stop in front of Old Pete's Crystal Saloon, Kathy discovered that she was out of breath, and her fingers ached from hanging on so tightly. She wanted more.

"Come on. I'll buy you a drink," said Kate, clapping the flat-brimmed hat onto her head.

Kathy wobbled into the dark coolness of the saloon like a sailor who has just left his ship. Wooden ceiling fans stirred the dry air above her head. A row of slot machines stood against one wall. Shelves lined the other walls, crowded with bits of junk that Old Pete had collected—rocks with fool's gold embedded in them, broken arrowheads, rusty mill gears, and pieces of peeling harness. A jukebox played country music softly from a corner in the back. Kathy climbed onto a stool beside Kate at the massive oak bar.

"Afternoon, ladies. What'll it be?" said Old Pete, wiping his hands on his dirty white apron.

"Double bourbon, neat," said Kate.

"Uh . . . root beer," said Kathy.

Pete washed and dried two glasses. He smiled, revealing a mouth full of night, marred only by two brownish teeth. He contemplated Kate and Kathy with friendly eyes, which too many years of sun had made wet and milky. "Mother and daughter, right?" he said.

"Guess again," said Kate.

Pete puckered his thin, dry lips. "Sisters?"

"Yeah, something like that." She winked and picked up their drinks.

Kate led Kathy to a table where they could watch the wind blowing dust along the wooden sidewalks outside. Kathy gazed at her as she took off her hat and tossed it easily onto the seat of the nearest chair. Was it true? Kathy imagined two people standing in a mountain stream. Would water that had touched her ankles touch Kate's someday?

"Who are you . . . really?" she asked softly.

Kate rubbed her thumb across the ridges of the bourbon glass. In the dim light of the saloon, her eyes were black lakes. "I swear to you, this is the truth. This morning I woke up just after sunrise, and I got dressed, and I went for a walk in Central Park. I thought, I'm thirty-seven years old, and it's June twenty-first, and twenty years ago to the day, I almost jumped off a cliff. I would have done it. Except a woman named Kate stopped me."

She lifted the bourbon and took a long swallow. "I thought about how fine the morning sun always looks, whether I see it on a wild lake or a row of city windows. And I knew it was time to go back, time to find you. I just knew what to do. Someday you will, too."

Kathy sipped at her root beer. It was too sweet, and not very cold. But her throat cried out for something to soothe away the sudden dryness. "Central Park? That's in New York, isn't it?"

Kate smiled and nodded. She slipped her wedding ring off and slid it across the table to Kathy. Kathy picked it up.

It felt heavy and warm and real. She closed her eyes and pressed the ring hard into her palm, trying to imagine a life that included things like Central Park and Manhattan and South American hats and a man who loved a woman who smoked cigars and carried a lavender silk handkerchief crumpled up in her pocket.

"Trust me, cookie," said Kate. "Your future is worth staying around for."

One tear, then another dropped onto the shining tabletop between Kathy's hands. She slid the ring back to Kate. "Promise?" she whispered.

"I promise."

Kate finished her bourbon in a long, last swallow, stood up, and grinned. "People are waiting for me," she said. "Good-bye, cookie. Take care of yourself." She turned and walked through the saloon doors to the street.

Several seconds passed before Kathy realized that Kate had forgotten her hat. "Kate!" she shouted. "Wait a minute!"

She shoved her chair back, grabbed the hat, and ran outside. She squinted up and down the sun-bleached street. But the wooden sidewalks and the dilapidated buildings stood deserted in the dry wind. The old dog had not stirred from his place in the middle of the road. The Jeep had disappeared. And Kate was nowhere to be seen.

Kathy turned the hat over and over in her hands. It was made of heavy wool felt, flexible but sturdy. Grimy fingerprints darkened the brim where Kate had habitually touched it. Inside the crown she found a small leather sticker that said *Producto de Buenos Aires* in shiny gold letters.

Just for fun, she clapped the hat over her own short curls. It fit perfectly. It smelled like peanuts and cigars and sweet, green grass.

Kathy smiled and stuck her hands in her pockets, wondering how far away New York City was.

CLOTAIRE'S BALLOON

As I approach my seventieth birthday, I find myself thinking more and more often of Aunt Henrietta and of the terrible thing my brother, Harry, and I did to her many years ago. Autumn has arrived, and I am growing old; perhaps that accounts for it. I have recently taken to spending an hour each morning on the porch. From my chair, I am occasionally lucky enough to see a balloon or two drift by, high and huge and wonderful, silent as clouds. Sometimes a breeze rattles the sumac leaves just the right way, or I catch a breath of apple cider on the air. Then I think perhaps I under-stand Aunt Henrietta as I never did when I was young. It isn't regret that I feel exactly—

something more like wistfulness. If only Henrietta had fully respected our childhood view of justice; if only Clotaire the balloonist had respected it a little less.

When Harry was eight and I was ten, our mother fell ill. At that time, we had wonderful lodgings in the city, in an ornate copper-roofed house that overlooked one of the parks. Harry and I were in the habit of sneaking about in the dark after we were supposed to be asleep. One evening early in spring, we peeked around the drawing room door-way. By the warm, uneven light of the fire, we saw Mother in her dressing gown and a quilt, seated in the largest and softest of the armchairs. Father sat beside her on the floor, leaning against her knees, an empty brandy glass tilted in his hand. I had never seen him sit on the floor before. Neither of them spoke or moved, but something about the way they stared into the flames made me feel quite empty and afraid. At that moment, I realized for the first time just how ill Mother really was.

Father's subsequent actions bore this out. In the middle of May we moved to a house in the country, where Mother spent most of her time lying in bed in a sunny room upstairs. The doctor gave orders that Harry and I were to see her no more than an hour each day and that even then we must be quiet and try not to excite her. This news terrified and infuriated me. In retribution, I took to breaking vases and scattering silverware about on the floor while Harry looked on in awe.

Two things happened because of this. First, Harry and I were firmly encouraged to stay outdoors most of the time, which is how we discovered Clotaire. And second, Father sent for his sister, Henrietta. So Clotaire and Aunt Henrietta entered our world together, the same way in which they departed from it.

One of those first country spring afternoons, as we stood with Father on the spacious lawn in front of our new house, Harry and I spied a balloon drifting high in the distance. I had never seen a balloon before and wasn't at all sure what it could be. I still remember just how it looked—shining silver, with a magnificent sun, moon, and stars about its circumference. It belonged to Clotaire, of course, though we didn't know it yet.

I jumped up and down, trying to see it better over the treetops, and cried, "What is it? It's so beautiful!"

"That's a balloon, Catherine," said Father. "There's a man hanging from it in a basket. He's taking a ride."

Harry leapt up as well, his cheeks all aglow, shouting, "Daddy, make him bring it here! I want a ride, too!"

Father laughed. His laughter in those days was brief and quiet and always made me think of Mother, lying pale in her bed. "I'm afraid he's too far away to hear us," he said, reaching down to tousle Harry's brown curls.

Harry squirmed but flashed one of those empty, sunny smiles of his. Father looked down at him, returned the smile rather stiffly, and said, "Come inside now, children. I have a surprise for you."

So, shielding our eyes and pointing at the receding silver balloon, Harry and I stumbled up the path to the front door and ran directly into Father's surprise—Aunt Henrietta. He hadn't told us he was expecting her, and I suppose we must have been playing and thus missed noticing the carriage that brought her from the station. At any rate, the unexpected sight of her ample, stalwart figure in the doorway affected us like a bolt of lightning from a cloudless sky. Harry and I were dumbstruck.

Tenacity and the smells of starched lace and lavender hovered around Aunt Henrietta, mothlike. We had never known her very well. She lived far away, visited our house only one week a year, and always brought with her a suit of scratchy new underwear for each of us. She taught at a private girls' school and raised large maroon roses in her spare time. I had two vivid memories of her, both of which at that moment crashed around inside my head like trapped finches. The first was of her slapping my hand as I reached for a third piece of cake at teatime. The second was of Harry's gurgling screams as she held him by the ear and washed his mouth out with laundry soap. He had made the mistake of saying aloud that he "didn't give a hoot about the heathen children in China," a turn of phrase that he had picked up from Father.

I suppose Harry and I must have looked a little bewildered as we stared up at her on the doorstep. She possessed hugely expressive black eyebrows, which she now raised into swooping arches that reached almost to the line of her stone-gray hair. "Children!" she said, her voice warm and sweet as those disgusting fig tarts she loved to eat. "How delightful to see you again."

Father put a hand on each of our shoulders. "Henrietta's come to stay with us until Mother gets better. Isn't that good of her?"

The eyebrows dropped, and a sort of smile crackled its way across Aunt Henrietta's powdery face. "Yes. I've come to help your father look after you for a little while. Won't that be nice?"

I suppose she thought she was doing the right thing. Perhaps she even thought this type of sacrifice would assure her of a place in heaven. After all, she was a solid and confident woman, with lucid ideas of the world. In all likelihood, it never occurred to her that she might only make matters worse by volunteering her services.

Harry and I were too young to see any of this, however. I knew only that Aunt Henrietta's presence at a time like this must mean that my mother was in terrible danger.

I started the new venture off well—with a bloodcurdling scream followed by, "I won't! I won't let you look after me. It's Mother's job. Leave me alone!" I ran straight across the lawn and into the woods, where I found solace in the rough branches of a maple tree. I cried until dark, when, as no one came looking for me, I climbed down and made my way home, feeling hungry and deserted.

Aunt Henrietta's presence in the house caused Harry and me to spend more time than ever out of doors. By the middle of July, when we first met Clotaire, we already knew exactly which trees in our woods were favored by cardinals and which by mourning doves; we had explored every turnstile and rock wall inch by inch and even befriended the great black bull who sometimes grazed in the field adjoining our raspberry patch.

Most important of all, we had learned to guess when the wonderful silver balloon was most likely to come drifting past. It had to be just the right kind of day. There had to be a line of dust shimmering like a halo on the road, and the sky had to look like Mother's blue crystal vase. Then, if luck and the high breeze came our way, we might catch a glimpse of the balloon, shining like an errant moon in the perfect sunlight. Now and then, it came so near to us that we could discern and wave to the man in the basket. Sometimes he waved in return, and sometimes he did not.

One afternoon during a fine round of our favorite game, missionaries and cannibals, we heard a strange sound. Harry and I stood still as rocks and listened. It was a noise like the beating of gigantic wings, accompanied by that odd roar and bellow that bulls sometimes produce when they are angry or afraid.

"Cathy, there's something in the field," whispered Harry. The dry willow branch he'd been using as a cannibal spear dropped unnoticed from his hand. That, and a slight croak in his voice, made the hair on my arms stand straight up beneath the sleeves of my blouse.

In a moment I saw what Harry was talking about—a huge, glowing thing that moved in waves just beyond the raspberries and the hedge. I got down on my hands and knees, crept through our secret hedge tunnel, and peeked out on the other side.

Harry was just behind me, not to be outdone by a girl. "Is it anything awful?"

I made room for him beside me. "Come and see."

Before us in that ordinary field was a sight that visits the dreams of an old woman to this very day. A tall but otherwise unremarkable chestnut tree grew there, and caught in its branches was the grand silver balloon. We saw immediately that the basket, all askew, hung empty. But directly beneath it a man lay in the grass, half propped on his elbows and looking very distressed indeed. Our friend the black bull pawed the ground no more than two yards away from him.

I stood up for a better look and, as sometimes happens with little girls, fell in love straightaway. I had previously thought that no one could possibly be more handsome and dashing than Father, but as I stood watching in the afternoon sun, I knew that Father had met his match. The fellow sported aviator's breeches and puttees and a lovely ivory-colored scarf. His eyes, the dazzling color of robins' eggs, were set in a strong, well-tanned face, and his hair and mustache gleamed like heaps of gold coins. Moreover, he seemed clearly in pain and danger. At once I felt capable of even the most arduous rescue. I floated in visions of befriending him and showing him off to Father and Aunt Henrietta, who seemed to care so little for me that they would let me sit in a tree by myself half the night.

"We've got to help him," I said. Bravely, and I now think

rather stupidly, I walked out into the field and flicked a stone at the bull's broad flank.

The bull looked around, distracted but unconvinced, and Harry yelped, "Don't, Cathy! He'll come after us."

"Nonsense," I said, hoping the handsome aviator could hear me. "The bull knows us. See?" And I clapped my hands and cried, "Shoo!" as loudly as I could.

Sometimes I think that God must station an angel on the shoulder of every little boy and girl and that only through that device does any child grow to adulthood. My angel must have been hard at work that day, for the bull turned and humped away as if it had been bitten by a fly.

"Shoo!" I said again, and it lumbered off even further.

Luminous with triumph, I turned to Harry. "Stand right here. Keep yelling 'shoo' and don't stop until I tell you to."

"But, Cathy . . ." he whimpered.

"Do it, or I'll twist your ear off." Poor Harry. I knew all of his weaknesses, even in those days.

So Harry crouched, all the little blue veins in his neck standing out, and screamed, "Shoo!" while I ran to the aid of the dashing young balloonist.

"Can you stand up?" I asked, breathless with a combination of excitements.

"*Oui*, mademoiselle, I think so," he replied. Oh, my knees nearly turned to butter.

I helped him up. But he winced and jerked when he tried to put weight on his leg, so I told him to lean on me. Lean on me he did, heavily and deliciously, as we hurried toward the gate in the hedge. He smelled wonderful, like cold air and lightning and peppermint.

When we stood safely on the other side of the gate, I called, "Run, Harry! Run!"

Screaming like a wounded pigeon, Harry tore through after us, even though the bull did not follow him, its attention having apparently wandered from stranded hero to succulent grass. That is how Harry and I at last made the acquaintance of Clotaire, the ace balloonist.

Later that very afternoon, as Clotaire sat before our fire soaking his foot and ankle in an Epsom salts bath, he said a thing which eventually changed our lives. He said, "I owe you a great debt. If there is ever any way in which I can repay it, you must tell me."

The peculiar look in his sky-blue eyes frosted the bones of everyone in the room, even Aunt Henrietta. Her twitchy eyebrows betrayed the nervousness that lay beneath her facade of haughty disapproval. It seemed as if a cold, sharp wind swept past the fire, for the flames wavered ever so slightly, though the day was still and mild.

An hour or so later, Father got out our touring car, which he showed off at every opportunity, and drove Clotaire to town. The moment they left the drive, Aunt Henrietta turned to us, her face ratlike in the dim light of the parlor, and said, "You're not to have anything more to do with that disreputable vagabond. Is that clear?"

I knew, of course, that Clotaire was a disreputable vagabond. It was the very reason I liked him so much. I already loathed Aunt Henrietta's imperious commands with such passion that any word from her had the power to make me do just the opposite.

I leapt to my feet and cried, "You're not our mother! You can't make us stop seeing him. I hate you. I hate you!"

For which I got my mouth washed out with laundry soap, while Harry stood by, unable to contain a quiet snicker or two. When the ordeal was over, I stumbled teary-eyed up the stairs, sneaked into Mother's room, and lay down beside her on the bed where she slept. I had a dream, which I remember even now. In it, Mother was well again, and we lived in the copper-roofed house that overlooked the park.

I made up my mind that I would do everything in my power to see Clotaire again, as a means of antagonizing Aunt Henrietta, if nothing else. Harry and I commenced spending virtually every waking hour out of doors, playing games of make-believe, always keeping a sharp eye out for Clotaire's mighty balloon.

We actually saw him three more times in the course of the next several months. The first two times, he drifted past above the treetops, waving to us. We leapt in the air and waved back to him. But we could not tell whether he called our names or not, for on both occasions he was ascending, and the balloon's burner roared and gushed flames like a dragon from a fairy tale.

The third time, however, the burner was silent, and Clotaire called down, "I will land in the field!" I was, of course, immediately transported to heights of perfect ecstasy.

I suppose I should tell you that many years later, when I was a full-grown woman, I had a suitor who owned a hot air balloon. I had it on excellent authority that this fellow was an adept balloonist and that his balloon, though it bore an unfortunate resemblance to a large Easter egg, was of the finest make. Yet I never saw him land where he really wanted to, and I never saw him attempt to take off or touch down without at least two strong men on the ground to help him. Whenever I recall Clotaire and that silver ship of his, I am astounded at the amount of control he seemed to have over it. Barring unexpected winds, and even then sometimes, he seemed perfectly capable of piloting his unwieldy craft without any aid whatsoever. That is precisely what he was doing on the occasion I now describe.

Harry and I had already reconnoitered the field once on this particular day, and we knew that the bull was nowhere to be seen. When Clotaire called down to us, we tumbled over one another like a couple of young rabbits as we dashed through the hole in the hedge to meet him. Quite clear of the chestnut tree, the balloon's varnished wicker basket thudded to the ground. Just as it began to rise again, Clotaire jumped out, carrying one of the anchor lines. In the blink of an eye, he pounded a long brass peg into the ground and tied the line to it. That was that, and nothing could have looked easier.

Clotaire said not a word as he stood gazing at us. His smile felt like a candle flame in the darkness, edged somehow with cold wind and thin air. It made me shiver, frightened me and delighted me all at once.

"Oh please, Mr. Clotaire," said Harry, clasping his hands before him, enthralled. "Please take us for a ride!"

I nudged him. "Don't be rude, Harry."

Clotaire rested one hand on his narrow hips and twisted the end of his golden mustache with the other.

"You might not like it. It's a strange world from those heights," he said. How chilly and wonderful those eyes of his were.

I remember my exact reply. Though I didn't know it then, I could not possibly have chosen more fitting words. "Oh, we'd like it fine, wouldn't we, Harry? We like strange worlds."

"Well, we shall see," said Clotaire, and he smiled again, as mysteriously as an Akkadian statue.

Clotaire lifted us over the rim of the basket as easily as he might have lifted two bags of thistledown and climbed in after us. He gave the anchor rope a surprisingly gentle tug; the brass peg pulled out, and we rose skyward.

For many years I have contemplated the rarities of that voyage. Some might be inclined to doubt their childhood memories of such events. But I can tell you this: I was born with a keen sense of what is real and what is not, and you may take my word for it. What Harry and I saw while peering over the edge of that basket was real.

Clotaire fired the burner, and we rose past the treetops, up into the cold blue cup of the sky. Not even the slightest breeze stirred the afternoon air, and when we stopped climbing we hung almost motionless, as if suspended on a string. Below us, we could see our house, the field, and the woods, and further off, the town.

Folding his arms across his chest, Clotaire said, "You do not yet understand about the worlds. Perhaps you never will, but I shall show you anyway."

He stretched out his hand and motioned toward the scene below. "This is one world." Then he snapped his fingers.

Harry and I sucked air as a shadow passed across the sun and a cold draft cut into our bones. I looked up, but I could see no clouds, no hawks or ravens, to account for the shadow. In a moment it was gone.

"And this is another world," said Clotaire.

Twenty-five or thirty cows had suddenly appeared in the field with the chestnut tree. Some of them had gotten through the gate and were grazing on our lawn, which looked unkempt and weedy. The house needed paint. "In this world, you never moved to the country," said Clotaire.

Snap. Shadows fluttered across the sun, and we spied a middle-aged woman and two children speeding down the drive in Father's motorcar. The noise of the engine floated up to us with eerie clarity. "A world in which your aunt became an avid traveler and learned tolerance from a Katmandese monk."

Snap. "A world in which the rules of civility are not quite the same." Two children looking very much like Harry and me came running across the field. We stared down at them, fascinated. Both of them wore fierce grimaces that revealed sharp yellowish teeth like those of wild rodents. The girl threw rocks at us with her powerful arms, and the boy carried a bundle of pointed sticks.

"Cannibal spears!" cried Harry. "*Real* cannibal spears!"

"I want to meet them," I found myself saying.

"Meet them?" The sky rang like a crystal bowl with Clotaire's clear laughter. "They would set upon you and kill you at once." He paused, then added, "Besides, there is something else. They are your counterparts. Touch them, and you cease to exist."

The boy threw a spear at us. It fell miserably short, but the inhuman rage on his face made me shudder. A great claw of terror tightened around me then, as if I stood alone in a dark hallway at night. "Take me home! Please, please take me home!" I cried.

Clotaire looked at me, his eyes blue suns, flaming and freezing. He smiled the Akkadian smile, snapped his fingers once more, and the old world lay spread below us again like a familiar quilt.

We descended. Clotaire jumped out, anchored the balloon as before, and lifted us from the basket. No one spoke at first. I watched the rise and fall of his broad shoulders as he breathed, in and out, in and out, the smells of peppermint and lightning.

It was Harry who broke the spell of silence. "Cathy! It's Aunt Henrietta! She's headed this way!"

The magic evaporated like kerosene on a hot sidewalk. Clotaire saluted us and said, "Adieu. I must be going, but we shall meet again."

Blood warmed my cold cheeks as I watched him vault back into the basket in a single liquid motion. Already, I heard Aunt Henrietta calling us, her voice as coarse and furious as a crow's. "Horrid children! No supper for you."

Harry tugged anxiously at my sleeve.

"Clotaire!" I cried. "Be careful. Don't let any counter-parts touch you."

Clotaire waved and pulled out the anchor peg. His words drifted down to us above the roar of the burner as the great silver balloon took to the air. "I have no counterparts."

For many nights after that, I lay in bed and tried to puzzle out a reasonable explanation for what I had seen on that peculiar ride. I never reached any very satisfactory conclusion. At any rate, all things, even my magical memories of Clotaire, grew unimportant in the weeks that followed, as the doctor, a man as large and plump as a thunderhead, came more and more often to our house. Sometimes he stayed the night. He and Father would emerge from Mother's room in the morning, faces gray and shoulders sagging. Aunt Henrietta would sit in the parlor with them while they drank strong tea or coffee (Father often added brandy to his) and spoke in whispers.

One afternoon well into autumn, the doctor arrived in a great flurry, his round face gleaming with sweat and his thin, white hair plastered to his forehead. When Aunt Henrietta opened the door, he said, "I got here as quickly as I could." Aunt Henrietta simply nodded and inclined her head in the direction of Mother's room, whereupon the doctor rushed up the stairs two at a time, huffing like a steam engine.

Harry and I raced after him, and would have followed him into Mother's room, only Aunt Henrietta grasped us by our collars and said, "You'll only be in his way." So we waited—I don't know how long, a few minutes perhaps—outside that door, which seemed larger and darker than it ever had before.

When the door opened at last, it was Father who stood there, a faceless silhouette in the afternoon sun that streamed through Mother's casement. He didn't say anything. He looked like a very old man, hunched and weary.

At once I felt as if I had swallowed a great chunk of emptiness. I whispered, "Mother!" and made for the space between Father and the doorframe, thinking to dart through and satisfy myself that my fears were unfounded. But he stopped me, of course. He took me firmly by the arm and closed the door behind him. He stood only a moment in the dark hallway. He never even looked at Harry and me. He simply turned his back and walked down the stairs.

On the day of Mother's funeral, I at first refused to wear the black dress that Aunt Henrietta purchased for me. Standing in my undershirt and bloomers, I tensed every muscle in my face and neck until my whole head shook and my eyes felt as if they would pop from my skull. "I won't! I want the red one with the flowers! Mother wants it that way!"

At first, Aunt Henrietta tried to reason with me. "Your mother had a good sense of what was proper. She'd have wanted you to show your sorrow."

"She hates black. You can't make me wear it!"

Henrietta had a gift for the deep stab and twist. She narrowed her eyes and said, "You had better come to terms with this, child. Your mother doesn't want anything. Neither does she hate anything. She is dead and beyond caring about you or anybody else."

At which point I threw myself on the floor and kicked and screamed until Aunt Henrietta finally got a shoehorn and raised welts on my bare backside with it. No one had ever actually beaten me before, and the whole experience left me so frightened and bewildered that I climbed into the black dress without another word. I tried to tell Father about it, but he had commenced drinking heavily on the day of Mother's death and didn't seem very concerned about my problems.

That night, after we had been put to bed, Harry crept into my room. I lay on the wide casement bench, unable to sit without great discomfort, and Harry huddled beside me. The moon was a bright crescent. Its faint light frosted the hills and whispered through the window onto our hands and faces.

"Shall we run away?" said Harry.

"How silly. We'd starve to death."

"But we can't stay here. She'll kill us."

I stared gloomily out at the night, wondering if perhaps Harry had a point. What happened next I would have been inclined to pass off as a dream, only Harry saw it, too. Far-off, above a distant wood, something large, round, and shiny appeared in the chilly sky, as if from nowhere. It took me a moment to recognize it as a balloon. I strained to make out what color it was, or to discern a familiar pattern of stars around its middle, but in that light I could be sure of nothing. We watched it drift for a minute or two, like a great steel ball somehow set free of gravity. Then it vanished. A prickle of fear and excitement ran through me. Harry and I exchanged one of those looks that signals a complex, shared thought—in this case, the memory of a summer fire guttering from an impossible, cold wind. *I owe you a great debt. If there is ever any way in which I can repay it, you must tell me.*

"Clotaire!" we whispered in unison.

We spent the night beside the open window, dozing by turns so that we would not miss Clotaire's balloon if it reappeared. After a time, the moon set, and the night grew dark and close, with only a sprinkling of stars to light it. Though I fought sleep, I must have drifted off anyway sometime in the small hours after midnight, for I awakened at dawn to Harry's urgent whispers and his tugging at my shoulder.

"It's him! It's him! Look, there's the balloon."

I rubbed my eyes and looked out across a windless autumn morning. The half-light robbed everything of color. The hills, the woods, the field lay cold and gray. A few birds twittered their morning songs. The sweet reek of neglected pomace in someone's cider press drifted up to us, mingled with leaf smoke. And there, splendid in the faded sky, hung the silver balloon. Blinking, I climbed up on the window ledge and waved wildly, shouting, "Clotaire! Wait, Clotaire."

When I felt certain he had seen me, I turned and bolted out the door and down the stairs. Harry ran after me, his bare feet slapping the polished wooden floors. We stood on the lawn in our nightgowns, waving and calling until the wicker basket touched ground and Clotaire stood before us.

"Hello, my friends," he said softly.

I looked into his face as steadily as I could, straightened my back, and said, "Sir, you made us a promise once."

He nodded and smiled a smile so faint that I could hardly be sure it was there.

"We want you to take someone . . ."

I was cut off by a shout from one of the upstairs windows. "Catherine! Harry! You shall be thrashed within an inch of your lives for this."

"I don't give a hoot!" shouted Harry, turning toward the house with his jaw thrust out and his hands on his little boy hips.

I squeezed my eyes shut until I saw stars. "I *said*, we want you to take someone away. To that last world . . . where the children are cruel and strong. Please!" I opened my eyes. "Take her away forever."

The sun had just broken over the horizon, and light flowed over Clotaire like a torrent of melted copper. His leather puttees, his sturdy breeches, his scarf, his hair, and even his beautiful face, all of him looked strong and hard as metal in that peculiar dawn.

He gazed down at us and said, "Be certain."

"We're certain!" we chorused.

Clotaire went to the wicker basket, opened a small wooden box, and took out a pistol. My mouth went dry. "What's that for?" I heard myself squeak.

Instead of answering, Clotaire grabbed me and held the pistol to my head. I fancied cold fingers closing around my heart. *I shall die,* I remember thinking. *And I shall probably go to hell.*

Aunt Henrietta burst from the front door of the house, her dressing gown flapping at her heels and her hair flying. "Save me," I prayed, "oh, Aunt Henrietta, save me!" as the muzzle of Clotaire's gun grew warm from the heat of my temple.

"How dare you!" she cried at first. Then she saw the pistol, and her eyebrows shot up, and she covered her mouth with her hands. "Oh, dear Lord," she said.

"Do as I say, and the child will not be hurt," said Clotaire. "Get into the basket."

"Help!" croaked Harry. "Oh, Father, help us." But Father lay drunk asleep in the far side of the house.

Aunt Henrietta climbed awkwardly over the wicker rim. "Sir, I beg of you, don't harm the children."

"Clotaire . . . I changed my mind. It's all right. You don't have to take her away." I was sobbing by then.

But Clotaire only laughed, a sound as hard and sharp-edged as glass. "You have made your bargain, my friend. It is past changing now."

He loosened his grip, gave me a small push in Harry's direction, and aimed the pistol at Aunt Henrietta. I doubt that I have ever felt so confused and powerless as I did then, watching Clotaire climb into the basket himself. Everything seemed wrong. I wanted him to take her away, and yet the execution of the act frightened me as much as the idea of her staying. I waited for a flood of satisfaction and release, but none came. Perhaps I had, on that distant autumn morning, my first glimmering of a difficult, grown-up fact. Outside of fairy tales, real justice is quite an elusive commodity.

"You had better keep quite still, madame," said Clotaire as he prepared to fire the burner.

"Where are you taking me?" whimpered Aunt Henrietta, her face the color of smoke.

Clotaire laughed, more musically this time, and said, "A place faraway but nearby, where things are not so very different. A place where you have no counterpart, never have had, and never will."

Then the burner roared. Flames erupted from it, and the silver balloon strained at its mooring. Aunt Henrietta, wild-eyed, clutched the rim of the basket. Clotaire shouted, "Heaven keep you, my friends." He pulled out the anchor line, and they rose—up, up, until at last, when they were smaller than a marble or an eye, they vanished.

Harry and I stood on the lawn in shocked silence. The smells of autumn leaves and fermenting apples washed over us as the birds began to twitter again.

Though sixty years have passed since then, that morning still looms in my mind like a shadow that crosses a field and changes the look of the ground in its path. Though I've led a fine life and don't hold much with wishful thinking, I can't help wondering about the other worlds. Which one would I live in today if Clotaire had said no to us, which one if Aunt Henrietta had not vanished in a balloon?

As things turned out, Father sent Harry and me away to separate schools after Henrietta's disappearance, probably because he thought it would be easier to drink himself into an early grave if there were no children about. He was dead before my twentieth birthday. Harry's gone now, too. He died last year from a heart ailment he never knew he had. As for me, I am left to carry on alone, since I never married. Though suitors courted me aplenty in my youth, none of them had what I was looking for—a certain unthinking impartiality, the ability to stand outside life's complications and laugh at them.

I never saw Clotaire again after that fateful morning. He disappeared with even more elegance than a puff of smoke. Sometimes, sitting here on the porch, remembering the old days, I long for one more glimpse of those robin's-egg eyes set so perfectly in that strong, tan face. I long to tell him that I understand things better now, understand about all the drunken Fathers, and all the Henriettas, and all the children who would be so fierce without them. In the best of all possible worlds, I would die with the scents of lightning and peppermint in this tired old nose. So I keep watch, and hope for one last look at Clotaire's balloon.

THE LILY AND THE
WEAVER'S HEART

When one-eyed Jacinth was ten years old and had just begun to weave tapestries, her mother took her and her two sisters to see the young men of Aranho set off in search of lilies. Jacinth pressed close to her mother as they stood in the noisy crowd at the edge of the village. Sunshine fell down like golden thread from a cloudless summer sky, and the thick grass of the meadows lay heavy with morning dew. Even the straw roofs of the houses and shops seemed bright and magical as Jacinth watched the parade of

Aranho's tall, handsome youths. Some of them had hair the color of flax, and others had hair as dark as ravens' feathers. Some sported the soft beards of early manhood, and others had shaven chins. They carried pouches of fragrant bread at their belts, and their knives and bows flashed gaily as they passed. They walked with their shoulders swaying, like men who are glad to be off and expect to return triumphant.

As she watched, Jacinth thought of the tapestry that hung unfinished on her loom at home. She had already woven into it a picture of her father grinding flour at his mill. Now she wondered if she could add this street, and the stone cottages, and the lines of proud young men striding away on their adventure.

Jacinth's older sister, Wynna, rose on her tiptoes, lifting both hands in the air. "There goes Sten!" she cried. "I see him!" Then louder, "Good luck, Sten. Bring me a lily. I'll be waiting."

From the far edge of the passing ranks, Jacinth could just make out a strong, tan arm waving in reply.

"What does a lily look like?" she asked, for in fact she had never seen one, and now she wondered if the lilies themselves could also be added to the scene in the tapestry.

"A lily looks like a bell," said her mother. "A very beautiful bell, yellow as fire or ripe peaches or the sun when it rises."

Jacinth frowned, trying hard to imagine such a flower. "Why does Wynna want Sten to bring her one? Just because it's pretty?" she asked.

Wynna looked down at her and smiled and ruffled her hair. "It's more than that," she said. "You'll find out some-day."

But Jacinth's other sister, Noa, who was fourteen and jealous of Jacinth's weavings, grinned wickedly and said, "No you won't. You'll never find out, old one-eye, because you're ugly, and nobody will ever want to bring *you* a lily!"

Jacinth ran her fingers across the familiar smooth skin where her left eye should have been. She remembered how her own reflection had made her run screaming from the still water of the millpond the first time she had seen it. And she knew Noa was right. She was ugly, and all the best things in the world, even flowers, were reserved for the beautiful. She bolted, covering her terrible face with her arms, heedless of her mother and Wynna as they cried, "Come back! Noa didn't mean it."

Jacinth ran alone through the deserted streets. The tears in her single eye dimmed the sun. The world, so bright with possibilities a moment before, seemed dark and frightening now. Rounding a corner, she lost her footing and hit the ground in a shower of dirt. Over and over she rolled, until she came to rest against a stone doorstep. There she lay, weeping. Dust stung her nose and throat. Her knees and elbows throbbed where she had scraped them in her fall. But the greatest pain of all lodged in her heart, where Noa's words repeated themselves insistently.

Just then, she heard a voice above her.

"Are you all right?"

Jacinth raised her head. From between the dusty strands of her hair, she saw a well-made shoe and the tips of two wooden crutches. Raising her head a bit further, she saw that the shoe fit a foot that was attached to a sturdy leg that was attached to a boy. The boy was clothed in brown wool—coarse, patched, and poorly spun, but clean. He had only one leg. Still, he was tall, and Jacinth could see that he was older than she, perhaps Noa's age.

"Are you all right?" he asked again.

She sat up and brushed her hair away from her face, waiting for his eyes to widen when he realized that she didn't look like other people. But his expression stayed the same. His pale brow was slightly furrowed, and his clear hazel eyes shone bright with concern.

With the back of her hand, she wiped the tears away. "Don't I scare you?" she said.

The boy looked puzzled. "Well, I was afraid you had hurt yourself."

"Oh, I did," said Jacinth, proudly displaying her bloody elbows.

The boy pursed his lips, which made him look much more grown-up than he really was. "Wait here," he said. "I'll get some water and a cloth. My master says it's bad to leave dirt in a scrape."

He turned and hobbled off into the house, which she now recognized as the shop of Bot the cobbler. A few minutes later, he returned with a crockery jug of cool water and a scrap of soft cloth. He stacked his crutches and, with surprisingly little trouble, sat down beside her on the doorstep. Gently, he took one of her elbows in his slender hands and began to clean the bits of gravel and blood from it.

"You're Jacinth, the miller's daughter, aren't you?" he said. "I've seen you before and I've heard my master talk about your weavings."

Jacinth nodded, suddenly afraid to speak for fear the tears would start again. If he had seen her before, that explained why her face hadn't frightened him.

"My name is Joth," he said. "I . . . I'm the cobbler's apprentice." Color rose suddenly in his cheeks, and he looked away from her, giving more attention to her elbow than it required.

She watched him silently, wondering at his strange behavior.

Joth dipped the cloth in the water and looked up again. "You didn't laugh," he said.

"Why should I laugh?"

Joth shrugged. "Most people think it's funny that a boy with only one foot makes shoes."

Something about Joth's words gave Jacinth a soft, warm feeling, as if a meadow full of buttercups had bloomed inside her. She looked at him, wondering if she could find some hint of a lie or a trick meant to make her trust him when she shouldn't. But his clear eyes seemed kind and honest.

At last she said, "I know. People think it's funny that a girl with only one eye should weave tapestries or go to see the lily hunt begin, too." She looked off toward the center of Aranho, where she knew the handsome young men must still be striding through the street on their way to the lilies that grew in the faraway forests. When she looked at Joth again, he was resting his chin in his hands and staring sadly away in the same direction.

Jacinth felt the tide of tears rising in her once more. "My sister says that no one will ever bring me a lily. She says I'm too ugly."

Joth sat up straight and smiled at her as softly as the last light of dusk. "I don't think you're ugly," he said. "I would bring you a lily if I had two good legs."

The strongest dike ever built could not have held back Jacinth's tears then. The hot, salty stream of them poured down her cheek as she stumbled up from the doorstep. She didn't know whether to hug Joth or run. She wanted to believe him. But no one had ever said such a thing to her before. What if he were lying? What if this were his way of making fun of her?

"Don't cry, Jacinth. Please don't," said Joth.

But she couldn't stop and, not knowing what else to do, she fled down the steps and into the street.

"It's true, Jacinth. You're not ugly," Joth called after her.

"I don't believe you!" she cried, without looking back.

Barely a week had passed when the first of the young men returned to Aranho, scruffy and mud-smeared but triumphant, bearing orange and yellow lilies like torches in their hands. That very evening, there was a proud, firm knock at the miller's door. Jacinth ran after Wynna as she hurried to answer it. There stood Sten, tall as clouds, the first stars strung like diamonds in the violet sky behind him. He smiled as he held out a flower on a leafy stem. Even the twilight could not rob the lily of its amber brilliance.

"Yes. Oh yes," whispered Wynna as she took it from him.

Jacinth watched as they walked arm in arm down the stone path to the gate, their bodies swaying together like stalks of wheat in the wind, and their faces aglow with mysterious joy. She thought of the scene in her tapestry—her father at his mill, the streets and the white cottages, the tall men with their knives and bows. She thought of Joth, and of what he had said to her. And for the first time, the deep winter coldness that would someday become old and familiar settled over her heart. For the first time, it occurred to her that perhaps there was no place at all in the tapestry for a boy with one leg, no place for a girl with one eye.

Soon enough, autumn came, and the citizens of Aranho prepared for the Great Wedding. The men stalked the fields in search of tender young deer, and the fattest pigs in the village were slaughtered. The women gossiped amiably among themselves as they sewed wedding costumes and cooked spicy dishes of squash, grain, and apples. Even the children ran errands and gathered branches laden with bright leaves for the marriage beds. Many of the men who had returned from the hunt with lilies that year were to be married. Sten and Wynna were among the new couples who danced in the wedding circle and drank from the high elder's cup of secret wine.

After the wedding, Sten took Wynna away to the cottage he had built for them. The miller waved good-bye, his shoulders square and a smile of pride on his face. His wife wept, though she could not say why. And Noa ran at the newlyweds' heels like a puppy, begging them to invite her often to the new house.

But Jacinth went off by herself and climbed quietly to her loft in the rafters above the millstones. She cut the

unfinished tapestry from her loom, rolled it up, tied it carefully with strong twine, and carried it to a dark corner, where
it stood untouched for many years thereafter.

Summer followed summer, and Jacinth watched the passage
of many lily hunts, many triumphant returns, and many
weddings. Three years after Wynna's marriage, there was
another knock at the door one midsummer's dusk, and then
Noa was gone, too, off into the world with a lily in her hand
and a man beside her. With each year, Jacinth felt herself
changing into a woman, cherishing a woman's hopes and
desires. But each year the chill in her heart grew a little
deeper, and the anger and energy with which she faced the
world grew a little stronger.

At last, the time for her own lily went by, as she had
feared it would, without event. After the Great Wedding
that year, she trudged back toward her father's mill alone,
tearing the garlands from her long hair and wishing she
could tear away the maiden's gown she wore as well. As it
happened, she passed the cobbler's shop on her way, and
there stood Joth on the doorstep. He had grown taller in the
time that had passed, and his kind hazel eyes were set in a
leaner face, with a jaw more firm and knowing than she
remembered. His crutches were propped beneath his arms,
and he held a jar of dark ale in his hands. He was smiling.

"Hello, Jacinth. It was a fine day for the wedding, wasn't
it?" he said.

"If you like that sort of thing," she replied.

Joth held out his jar. "Will you have a drink of ale with
me, to wish the newlyweds well?"

But Jacinth's frustrations swept over her head like angry water, and she shouted, "How can you be so gay about it? Don't you see that there's no place for us here? Half the roads in the world are closed to us for no good reason at all!"

She started to run, her head awhirl with her own cares. But the crash of breaking crockery in the road behind her made her stop. She turned.

There lay the ale jar, a heap of shattered fragments in a dark brown pool. Joth's eyes were wet and bright, and his body as taut as a bowstring. "Then what are we to do?" he cried. "Lie down and die? I would rather make my own roads!"

He spun on his one leg and disappeared into the cobbler's shop.

All through the smoky autumn and the winter, Jacinth spent her days alone in the meads and thickets, foraging for bark and stones and roots with which to dye her yarns. At night, she lit candles in the chilly loft and sat at her loom while the wind rushed across the meadows and through the brittle trees outside. She worked as if a demon lived inside her. Her fingers grew stiff and raw, and thin lines creased her forehead from the effort of peering at close work with her single eye. Only when the sun rose and the candles had turned to stubs did she ever give in to sleep, for she hated the dreams that came to her, and awoke from them weeping.

The tapestries she wove in that long, dark season became her only respite. When her heart thrashed like a desperate bird, when she could not face her lonely bed, she wove tapestries, and they were like no others. They were filled with all the power, beauty, and pain that had no other way of escaping from her. She spun fabulous worlds, told impossible tales, and the people she wove danced and wept as if they were alive.

When the weather began to soften and the air to grow rich with the smells of green buds, a merchant came to the miller's door. He said that in his village, which lay two days' ride to the west, he had heard rumors of the one-eyed weaver of Aranho. He asked to see the tapestries, and when Jacinth showed them to him, he bought several, paying her well for them.

The next afternoon, Jacinth sat in the dappled sunlight beneath a willow tree and bounced Wynna's children on her knee. They were used to her and thought nothing of the fact that their aunt had an eyeless cheek. They spoke to her and laughed as if she were anyone else. Jacinth felt the fragrant spring breeze touch her. She thought of her good fortune with the merchant, and of the places and futures she had woven into the tapestries. It came to her that perhaps Joth was right. Perhaps even a woman with one eye, if she was strong enough, could make her own roads.

That summer, Jacinth watched a man build a new cottage. As she observed him, she took careful stock of the money she had made from the sale of her tapestries. When the man was finished and she had learned all she could from watching him, she set about making a cottage for herself. She chose a small piece of land near a creek on the outskirts of Aranho and she bought a few tools. From a glazier who lived nearby, she purchased six round pats of thick, bubbly glass with which to make a window.

The work of building a house was not easy. The sun reddened her skin, and the tools slipped sometimes and bit into her weary hands. She made mistakes, for she had to learn as she went along. At first, the villagers laughed and jeered at her because it was unheard of for a woman to build her own house. They said that Jacinth must wish she were a man. Noa ordered her to stop, for her actions were unseemly and embarrassing. But Jacinth only smiled and went on.

When it became clear that her project would succeed, the villagers stopped laughing and grew sullen. Still she worked, and before the summer ended, she moved her loom from the loft above the millstones to her own snug cottage with its thick window, straw roof, and warm hearth. In a corner by the fire, she propped the unfinished tapestry she had cut from the loom so many years before. There it stood mutely, where she could always see it.

By the time the leaves changed color, the world seemed a different place to Jacinth. Her senses, which had for so long been deadened by her sorrow, began to awaken again. When she wandered in the groves and fields in search of dyestuffs, the songs of hidden birds swept over her like wind, and the autumn sun made her body tingle with pleasure. The smells of soil and ripe fruit and leaf mold no longer made her think of wintry death. Instead, they seemed a part of something wonderful and vast, a ritual of the earth much larger and more lasting than that of men.

She gathered berries and insects and flowers that she had never noticed before, and the dyes they yielded gave her a palette like that of no other weaver in the land. When winter came, all the corners and nooks of her house were stuffed with skeins of yarn in every color, ready to be threaded into warp and weft and woven into the images of Jacinth's heart.

While the snow fell and the sharp wind blew it into drifts, Jacinth sat at her loom. She worked long hours every day, stopping only when she needed firewood or food, or when her eye grew too tired to decipher the threads before her. In the cheerful warmth of the cottage, her fingers stayed supple much longer than they had in the drafty mill loft. From dawn till dusk, the well-made window let in winter's pale light, which served her much better than the flames of tallow candles had. Jacinth finished tapestry after tapestry, each one alive and powerful in its own right, each one an improvement on the last.

When the ice and snow began to melt and the first green shoots of grass pushed up from the muddy fields, three men came to Aranho asking for the one-eyed weaver. Two of the men were ordinary merchants who had driven donkey carts from villages in the nearby countryside. But the third man wore rich clothes and rode a glossy black horse.

"I am here in the service of a wealthy nobleman," he said. "My master asked me to pay you for some tapestries to warm the stone walls of his house."

Jacinth shrugged and spread her winter's work in the sun for the men to see. Then she watched with her arms crossed and her lips pressed tight together as they argued and compromised with one another over who was to get which of the pieces. A part of her felt elated and triumphant at this evidence of her success. But the old bitterness still lay inside her like a small, sharp jewel. And the part of her that cherished it could not forget that although men might desire her tapestries, they had never desired the woman who wove them.

The next week, Jacinth took her dye pot to a sunny glade near the creek. She filled the pot with water and set it to boil over an open fire, then went about gathering enough meadow flowers to make a good yellow dye. As she stooped to pick a handful of wild mustard, she heard someone whistling in a tuneless and preoccupied way among the linden trees that grew by the water. She stood up to see who it could be, and the whistling stopped.

"Jacinth, is that you?" someone called.

She recognized Joth hobbling toward her over the muddy spring soil. She sighed, for in a small, mean way, she resented the fact that no one except another cripple ever took the trouble to greet her with such kindness. Nevertheless, the air was so sweet and warm and the songs of the robins so bright that she made up her mind to be friendly in return.

"Hello," she said. "What brings you to the creek today?"

"Cobbler's reeds," he said, standing still before her with the sun in his hair. "Old Bot sent me to see if there will be enough cobbler's reeds this year to make shoes for those who can't afford leather."

Jacinth dropped the mustard flowers into her basket, and she and Joth wandered toward the waiting dye pot. "And what will you tell him? Will there be enough reeds?"

Joth nodded. "A sizable crop. And what brings you to the creek?"

"Yellow dye." Jacinth motioned toward the flowers that lay in her basket like a mound of captured sunlight, bees whirring above them in a single-minded search for pollen.

When they reached the dye pot, Jacinth shooed the bees away and tipped the basket up. Joth, with his crutches tucked under his arms, scooped the fragrant harvest into the boiling water for her. He lay down in the grass and, chewing on a single leafy blade, watched her stir the dye with a stick and carefully add unspun flax to it. The water hissed and bubbled.

In the drowsy afternoon, Joth began to talk, slowly and idly, laughing now and then, about leather and lasts and awls, and about his childhood in the house of Bot the cobbler. Much to her astonishment, Jacinth found herself speaking in return. She told him about the little round beetles from which she made her best blue dye, and about the long winter of weaving and the light that came through her window.

Shadows were thin and the air had grown chilly when Joth looked down at his hands and said, "I'm sorry. You must think I'm a silly fool to lie in the grass all day and bother you when you are busy with your work."

Jacinth glanced at him and smiled, for his solemn frown looked out of place beside the foxtails that rode here and there among the strands of his shining hair.

"Not at all," she said. "No one has ever spoken to me that way before. And I've never spoken to anyone as I have to you just now, except perhaps in dreams." She felt her cheeks redden and she brushed her face with the full sleeve of her blouse, as if to wipe away steam from the dye pot.

Joth reached for his crutches and began the slow process of standing up. Jacinth offered him her arm, and he leaned against her as he rose. She felt the warmth of his strong hands on her shoulder and remembered how gently he had cleaned the gravel from her elbows when they were children.

"I'll be back a week from today," he said, "to check the reeds again. Perhaps I'll see you."

"Perhaps," said Jacinth, and she waved to him as he started across the field toward Aranho. When he had dwindled to a small, limping figure in the distance, she sat down by the fire and picked up a stick. Staring after him, she stirred the ruddy embers beneath the dye pot into a confusion of hungry flames.

They met many times in the field beside the creek that spring. Joth came more and more often to check the reeds, and Jacinth found reasons, no matter how small, to gather whatever flowers were blooming in the meadow. In the long afternoons, only the birds and the buzzing insects heard the murmur of two human voices in the glens and linden groves. As spring turned into summer, Joth and Jacinth spoke to each other first like gregarious children, then like old friends. By and by, they spoke almost without words.

The first month of summer was nearly through when Jacinth recognized the longing that welled up in them both. They lay beside the creek, propped on their elbows, facing each other. Joth tickled her lips with a long blade of timothy. Then softly, with his fingertips, he stroked her hair and her cheek and the smooth hollow above it, which no one but Jacinth had ever touched before. She closed her eye and felt the large wetness of tears forming there and did not know whether joy brought them, or confusion, or knowledge that the time was not yet right.

Jacinth caught his hand and wove her fingers through his. "Though I wish it were otherwise," she said, "we must be patient awhile longer."

A shadow fell across Joth's face, and his eyes grew dark for a moment. "Have I overstepped myself?" he asked. The question seemed simple, but in the sound of his voice and the way he held his head, Jacinth saw that he had left much unasked. She held his hand tighter.

"No, dear Joth," she said. "You are like the sun to me. No day seems whole without you anymore. No task seems meaningful. But there is something I must do first." She gazed at him, thinking of the tapestry, of the lily she had never received, and of the bitterness that lingered in spite of her love for Joth. From a thicket across the stream came the hollow cry of a short-eared owl.

So it came to pass that in the early summer Jacinth prepared to join the lily hunt. She told no one the exact nature of her plan, not even Joth, though she was sometimes certain he had guessed it. She made herself a pair of stout, coarse trousers and a sturdy jerkin the color of thick forests. The smith of Aranho gazed at her quizzically when she bought a tempered dirk from him; the fletcher frowned at her request for a bow and a quiver of ashwood arrows. But in the end, her gold was as good as anyone else's, and they accepted her money though she offered no explanations. Last of all, she straightened her back and strode into the shop of Bot the cobbler, as if she were any other customer.

Bot was old, and his hands too gnarled for proper cobbling, so Joth did the fine work while Bot cut leather and cajoled his customers. Jacinth ordered a pair of tall leather boots from him, finished with beeswax to keep out the cold and damp.

"I'll be walking a long way," she said as Bot measured her. "Sometimes through deep mud and sometimes over rocks."

She looked up and saw Joth watching her as he worked at his last, one eyebrow raised. Her heart quickened with fear and excitement at the thought of the task she was about to undertake.

At last the appointed morning arrived. In the chill light of dawn, Jacinth dressed carefully, as she imagined a knight might dress before battle, pale and filled with the need to trust something larger than herself, a set of rules, a ritual made right by centuries of practice. She tugged the new boots over her calves, slipped the dirk through her belt and the quiver over her shoulders. Then she knotted a bag of journey bread at her hip, took up her bow, and started down the road to Aranho, looking neither right nor left.

By the time she reached the village, a crowd of young men had already gathered in the square, all laughter and nerves in the first copper light of the sun. As she approached, a hush fell over them. The muscles of her stomach tightened as she waited to see what would happen.

"What are you doing here, one-eye, dressed up as if you were a man?" asked one of them.

Jacinth fought the old fury and pain as she replied quietly, "I am walking with you to the forest."

Several of the young men cried out at once. "But you can't! . . . But you're a woman! . . . You have no right to join in the lily hunt!"

Jacinth laid her hand on her dirk. "I have a right to walk wherever I please, whenever I choose. And if any of you think otherwise, then I invite you to stop me, at the expense of your own blood or mine."

A low muttering rippled through the crowd, and Jacinth tightened her grip on the dirk.

At that moment, a clear voice cut across the morning air, as sharp as the cry of a meadowlark. There stood the high elder of Aranho, a man who was old long before Jacinth or the lily hunters had been born. He rested withered hands on thin hips and said, "Who among you ever offered her a lily?"

Silence fell on the crowd once more as men looked away across the fields or watched their own feet shuffling uneasily in the dust. No one answered.

"Then none of you has the right to stop her," he said, standing squarely, like a battle-scarred hound who is well aware of his own strength. After a moment, he squinted at Jacinth and smiled through his wrinkles. She nodded her thanks.

Without another word, the young men made way for her, and she took her place among them. She stood as straight and tall as she could, resisting the urge to paw the ground like a nervous horse as she waited for the procession to begin. Neither did she turn her head, searching for particular faces in the growing crowd of spectators, as some did. Her cheeks burned, for she knew how she must stand out among the sturdy hunters. She imagined the citizens of Aranho whispering about her, snickering behind their hands, as they had done so many times before.

Though it seemed to her that hours passed, the sun was still low in the sky when the march began at last. They headed east, toward the sea and the deep forests.

As they approached the last stone cottage before the village gates, she heard someone call her name. From the grassy verge beside the road, her sister Wynna waved, children clinging to her skirts as Jacinth had clung to her own mother's skirts long years before. Beside her stood Joth, looking tall and strong in spite of the crutches tucked under his arms. Jacinth slowed her vigorous pace and blinked, for in all the years she had known him, Joth had never gone to watch a lily hunt begin.

"Good luck!" called Wynna.

Jacinth raised her hand to return Wynna's greeting, but her gaze never left Joth's face. He was smiling, and the smile illuminated him as if the day's soft yellow sun had risen from the horizon of his own heart. Its light crept into every corner of her, no matter how deep the shadows, and courage came with it.

"I'll be back soon," she cried. "I promise you!"

Then the tide of marching hunters swept her up, and the journey began in earnest.

They followed the road toward the east, traveling across grassy plains that ran unbroken for miles and miles. For two nights, Jacinth camped alone, ahead of the others. They would have nothing to do with her once the high elder had been safely left in the distance. On the first day's march, some of them made a game of throwing pebbles at her so that she was forced to choose between endless small bruises and solitude. In her pride and pain, she took advantage of the fine boots Joth had made for her and strode ahead smiling grimly while the strong young men of Aranho trudged along on tired and blistered feet. A bitter satisfaction filled her, for she had been forced to accept solitude many times over in her life. It was nothing new to her. No matter, she thought, as she lay beside her small fire. She tried to dream only of Joth and the lilies, but the night songs of toads and owls pounded down on her like cold, lonely rain, and she cried in her sleep, her fingers clenched white around the handle of her dirk. For it did matter. It mattered as much as it always had.

Jacinth knew nothing specific about where the lilies might be found. She suspected that some of the other hunters had received instructions from those who had gone before. But even if that was true, none of them would have shared such manly secrets with a woman—particularly one so proud and hideous. She knew only that lilies favored damp, shady places, loamy ground near bogs or the margins of deep forest ponds. She knew also that the forests lay in the low hills that separated the meadowlands from the eastern sea. When the hunters began their march from Aranho, the wooded coastal hills lay far off in the blue distance. But every day they grew closer, until on the third morning the faint smells of leaf mold and pitch and the vast, wet sea awakened Jacinth from her troubled sleep.

She sat up at once, sniffing the air. The sun had just risen. Birds twittered sleepily, and somewhere in the shadowy grass a cricket still chirped. She looked into the windless sky, and eagerness surged through her as she realized that before this day was over she might well be holding a lily in her own hands. She scrambled into her boots, picked up her weapons, and started down the road.

Before noon, the road had become a narrow path among tall, leafy trees. Jacinth sat down to rest a moment. She wondered whether to follow the road until it disappeared entirely or strike out on her own. The thought of leaving the traveled way frightened her, for she had never been in a real forest before. Strange, bright flowers pushed up through the carpet of fallen leaves and needles; shining beetles crept over the rocks. She did not know what animals might lurk among the trees.

Suddenly, as if fierce bears and wild pigs had leapt from her mind into the woods, she heard the sharp snap of a dry twig.

She jumped up, drawing her dirk, and found herself staring into the grimy face of a lily hunter. His fair hair stood up in dusty spikes, and the lines of dirt around his mouth flowed into an arrogant grin.

"You slept too late, one-eye," he said, hooking his thumbs into his belt. "My friends and I will take all the lilies, and we'll be on our way back to Aranho before you even know where to look. Then maybe you'll understand your place in the world."

Jacinth's heart sank like a rock tossed carelessly into an icy stream. The long winters of lonely weaving washed over her, and she thought of the unfinished tapestry, of returning to Joth empty-handed and broken beyond saving.

The young hunter must have seen the terror in her face, for he leaned back and roared with ugly laughter. "That's what you get!" he shouted jubilantly. "That's what you get for trampling the old laws!"

She stared at the dirk in her hands, its cool blade gleaming in the sunlight. *The old laws!* a voice inside her screamed. *The laws that say there is no place for a one-eyed weaver or a cobbler with one leg!* In her fury she grasped the blade and crushed it until she felt the metal bite through her palm. Blood ran in scarlet rivulets down her wrist.

Through a haze of pain and passion, Jacinth watched the young hunter turn and swagger off down the path, his shoulders still jumping with laughter.

"I make my own roads!" she cried. "I make my own roads!"

But if he heard her at all, he gave no sign of it.

She sat down on a flat stone and bound her hand as well as she could with a strip she tore from the hem of her shirt. After a time, the anger and trembling left her. A cold, desperate courage replaced it. Let the menfolk of Aranho seek lilies where they always had! The woods were thick and huge and full of places where no human being had ever walked before. She would find her own lilies, or she would die in the attempt. She stood up, straightened her back, and plunged into the forest.

She followed the contours of the land ever upward, leaving a trail for herself by cutting notches into the tree trunks at regular intervals. The farther she went into the woods, the larger the trees became, and the thicker the undergrowth. Spiral ferns snatched at her arms and legs, and bloated insects stung her face. She tripped over roots and waded through thick, slimy mud. She tried not to notice the eerie cries and thrashings of the unknown creatures around her, tried to ignore the swollen fungi that sprang up in rank profusion on the damp forest floor.

Late in the afternoon, when dusk had already descended around her, she came to a place where the land sloped down in all directions. She stood at the base of an ancient maple tree and turned slowly. She had arrived at the crest of a hill. Yet the trees were so tall and closely spaced that she could see nothing, so she laid down her bow and set about climbing the maple.

Its trunk was almost as big around as her father's largest millstone, and the branches hung far above her head. But the maple had stood in the forest for many long years, and its bark was thick and full of ridges. By stretching and straining and planting her supple boots carefully in these small footholds, she gained the lowest branch. Higher and higher she climbed until at last she stood erect in leafy sunlight far above the other trees. She clung to the branches for a moment, giddy with the view that spread below her. As the sun sank lower and the land cooled, a spicy wind flowed out of the forest toward the sea, which lay like a bolt of blue-gray satin on the eastern horizon. The trees marched down to it, thronging over the hills until they reached the broad, white shore.

A valley lay at the southeastern foot of her vantage point. The valley cradled just what Jacinth had hoped to find—a small, glassy lake, fringed on one side by a marsh. Loons flew above it in profusion, making ready for the night. Their laughing cries floated up whenever the wind dropped. Jacinth's blood sang like the strings of a well-tuned harp. The land, the sea, the wind spoke to her like old friends, and she knew deep within her that if she could reach that lake, she would find the key to a new life for herself and Joth; she would finish the tapestry and pluck it from her loom in jubilation at last. She took one last worried glance at the sinking sun, then scurried down the tree and trotted off through the dusky undergrowth toward the southeast.

She knew full well that she oughtn't travel at night, but she was loath to camp in the closeness of the forest, which clung to her and made her feel as if she walked through invisible cobwebs. She ached to reach the lake and the wide sky above it. As the light waned, color seeped out of the

woods until at last Jacinth saw only gray shapes everywhere, some deeper in shadow than others. Huge dusty
moths flew out of the ferns as she passed. Mist hovered
near the ground. She stumbled frequently, splashed
through hidden puddles, and stirred up ashlike swarms of
stinging insects. At first she slapped at them, but there were
far too many. Before long, her face was swollen and tender
from their venom. Still, she pushed on with as much speed
as she dared, stopping only to cut marker notches in the
trees, for there were noises everywhere in the brooding
darkness around her. Wherever the forest drew back
enough to admit the sky, she saw the first stars twinkling.
Sometimes she heard the calls of the loons as they flapped
across the violet evening to the safety of the lake. Just a little
farther, she thought. And she forced herself onward.

Though she could not yet see the lake, she could
already smell its rank dampness, hear the splash of fish and
loons on its wide surface, when she realized that something
was tracking her. She stood still and listened. In the under-
brush to her right, leaves crackled for an instant, then
stopped. Jacinth felt her blood, like hot oil, surging through
her knees and wrists, boiling in her throat and in the knife
cuts on her hand. She took the bow from her shoulders and
nocked an arrow slowly, as if in a long, uncomfortable
dream. She squinted into the darkness, straining to discern
the creature that must be lurking there. With only one eye,
she was not certain that she could hit her target even if she
could see it. Images of huge black bears and slavering
wolves leapt through her mind. The bow and the ashwood

arrow trembled in her hands as if they had nerves of their own. The woods seemed choked with the silence of waiting. Then she heard it again—the crackle of dead leaves under the weight of something large.

She whirled blindly toward the sound. Almost with surprise, she heard the twang of her bowstring, felt the sting of the wobbly arrow as its shaft and stiff feathers rushed past her left wrist. With a sharp thunk the arrow hit something substantial—either tree trunk or bone. It shivered musically in its unseen mark.

From the deep shadows came a cry of indrawn breath. And an instant later a quavering voice called, "Don't! Don't kill me! I'm alone."

Jacinth lowered her bow in astonishment. "Show yourself," she shouted into the gloom, half relieved and half furious.

With great crashing and crackling, a man emerged from among the trees. By the light of the stars and the rising moon, she could see that he held his hands out at his sides, palms up and empty. When he stood within a few steps of her, she recognized him as the arrogant lily hunter who had confronted her on the road. He had no arrow in him.

"I'm . . . I'm sorry," he stammered. "I . . . we've found hardly any lilies where the elders told us to look. Only two or three. There's not enough food. The hunting's been bad, and today a bear killed the baker's son. It was my idea to follow you. Because of what you said . . . that you make your own roads. I thought . . . I thought you might . . ."

His voice trailed off into self-conscious silence. By the faint, cold light of the moon, she saw that he was nearly weeping with fatigue. His face and hands were covered with dark scratches, and mud smeared his clothes.

Jacinth stared at him dumbfounded. She felt as she had when, as a child, Noa had blindfolded her and forced her to walk across a narrow, bouncing plank. They were playing in the rafters of the mill. Noa told her that the plank stretched high above the grinding stones, and that if Jacinth slipped, she would fall to a grisly death. Jacinth had started across the plank, her knees quaking and fear clawing at her insides like a wild animal. Midway she had fallen, and in the moments after she realized that Noa had lied, that the plank was only a few hands above the floor, she had felt just as she did now—betrayed, foolish, and ashamed of her gullibility.

All her life she had revered the lily hunt, connecting it with the mystery of that summer dusk when Sten had come for Wynna, attributing to it all the magic of hard-earned passage from a child's thralldom into the independence of maturity. But now the blindfold was ripped away. So this was the lily hunt! The old men of the village told the young men exactly where the prizes were to be found and what to expect along the way. If it had ever been a true test of courage and resourcefulness, it was no longer. The brave lily hunter who stood before her was just a boy, whining because he'd had an unexpected taste of manhood and didn't like the flavor. If he found a lily tomorrow, he would think of it as something he deserved, and probably sulk because it hadn't come more easily. If he ever became a man, what happened in these woods would have precious little to do with it.

Like a cave dweller who has climbed up through bleak caverns and seen the sun for the first time rising at her door, Jacinth now realized that the thing she sought had been there all along. She had convinced herself that without the flower talisman, she could never be a woman. She had spent her life in bitter longing because her peers had judged her by her eyeless cheek and found her wanting, and so, she thought, withheld from her the thing she desired most. All along, the lily had been inside her. And Joth, dear Joth, who had always known, waited patiently while she found her own road to it.

In the forest night, Jacinth threw back her head and laughed, more freely and joyously than she ever had before. The lily hunter shuffled his feet and watched her nervously as if she had gone mad, which only made her laugh even more. Her ribs ached, and her voice was hoarse by the time she stopped.

She smiled at the disheveled young man and shook her head. "All right then. If you'd like, we can share a fire tonight," she said, wiping the tears of mirth from her eye.

She looked up into the starry sky. "Do you see those loons?" she asked. "They live on the lake that lies just ahead of us. Stand still a moment and you can hear the water lapping at its banks. It's the kind of place where lilies are likely to grow. I plan to camp there."

Without another word, she turned and started through the dark woods again. The young hunter breathed deeply, dragged the back of his hand across his forehead, and trotted after her.

Before another hour had passed, the trees suddenly gave way to open meadow. Jacinth stood at the edge of the clearing, silenced by its beauty. The stars and the full moon hung like pearls in the deep sky. The surface of the lake shivered with cool light. Loons laughed softly from the safety of the cattails, and frogs and crickets warmed the night with their songs. But most wonderful of all were the lilies.

Mingled with the grasses, the lilies grew in rich abundance, their blossoms waving in the soft breeze like the bright faces of a throng.

"Silver!" the young man murmured beside her. "They're silver!"

And indeed it was true. Even in the moon's chilly light, Jacinth could see that the graceful lily trumpets bore no hint of orange or yellow. She laughed once more, softly this time, with wonder. She had made her own roads indeed. And they led to lilies such as no one in Aranho had ever seen before.

Jacinth and the young hunter made a fire, caught fish and roasted them without speaking, for the lake and the lilies and the light of the moon cast a spell that words would have broken. When the fire had died to red coals and the hunter lay beside it, twitching in his sleep, Jacinth rested in the soft grass and looked up at the stars. Dearest Joth, she thought. I will be home soon, and I will bring with me greater treasure than I had ever hoped to find.

In the morning, Jacinth left the hunter where he slept. She broke off a piece of journey bread and laid it in the grass beside him, as a sign of goodwill. Then she went about the happy business at hand. First she wove a basket from cattails. Root and all, she dug a single silver lily decked with two blossoms and several buds. This she planted in the basket with good loamy earth and water from the lake. With her bow slung across her shoulders and the lily cradled in one arm, she set off through the forest again, back the way she had come, following the notches she had cut into the trees.

By afternoon, she reached the main road. Her heart was light as thistledown as she strode along, humming a tune and wondering idly what kinds of dyes could be made from the unfamiliar flowers she passed.

Once, she heard voices. She crouched behind a boulder as two lily hunters trudged up the road toward the forest.

Jacinth kept silent until they had passed. Then she continued toward home, whistling.

She reached Aranho on the evening of the eighth day. Though she was tired and hungry and her body ached, she stepped proudly along the main street. The lily, snug in its basket of soft, moist earth, glowed softly in the dusk, still as fresh as it had been on the morning when she dug it. As she passed, curious citizens thrust their heads from windows or walked out onto their doorsteps to whisper with their neighbors. It was not the usual greeting reserved for the first returnee from the lily hunt. Nevertheless, she noticed the onlookers much less than she noticed the familiar stone houses and straw roofs. Whatever its shortcomings, Aranho was her home, and she was glad to be back.

Through the purple twilight she marched to the door of the cobbler's shop. Joth opened it as she raised her hand to knock. His face was as luminous as the lily.

"I'll tell you a story," he said as they stepped into the street on their way to Jacinth's cottage. "About a lame cobbler who fell in love with a one-eyed weaver."

She laughed. "I already know that one. I'll tell you one even better. About a weaver who traveled all the way to the sea and back just to find out that all she really wanted was to marry a cobbler and live the rest of her life in the town where she was born."

Joth gazed at her merrily as he swung along on his crutches, his eyebrows arched in mock surprise. "All the way to the sea?"

"Oh yes. It took that great a distance," she replied.

And they laughed and sighed together as Jacinth began to tell him all that she had seen.

Later, they lay together on the soft straw of her pallet before a small fire in the house she had built with her own hands. She held Joth close to her as he slept. She gazed drowsily at her warm, familiar room. There was the loom, and the thick window above it, and the baskets of many-colored yarn. There was the lily. She would plant it tomorrow, in the cool sheltered light on the east side of the cottage. In a shadowy corner, the unfinished tapestry stood waiting, as if today were no different from any other.

Quietly, she rose and began to thread it back onto the loom.

CAT IN GLASS

I was once a respectable woman. Oh yes, I know that's what they all say when they've reached a pass like mine: I was well educated, well traveled, had lovely children and a nice husband with a good financial mind. How can anyone have fallen so far, except one who deserved to anyway? I've had time aplenty to consider the matter, lying here eyeless in this fine hospital bed while the stench of my wounds increases. The matrons who guard my room are tight-lipped. But I heard one of them whisper yesterday, when she thought I was asleep, "Jesus, how could anyone do such a thing?" The answer to all these questions is the same. I have fallen so far, and I have done what I have done, to save us each and every one from the *Cat in Glass.*

My entanglement with the cat began fifty-two years ago, when my sister, Delia, was attacked by an animal. It happened on an otherwise ordinary spring afternoon. There were no witnesses. My father was still in his office at the college, and I was dawdling along on my way home from first grade at Chesly Girls' Day School, counting cracks in the sidewalk. Delia, younger than I by three years, was alone with Fiona, the Irishwoman who kept house for us. Fiona had just gone outside for a moment to hang laundry. She came in to check on Delia and discovered a scene of almost unbelievable carnage. Oddly, she had heard no screams.

As I ran up the steps and opened our door, I heard screams indeed. Not Delia's—for Delia had nothing left to scream with—but Fiona's, as she stood in the front room with her hands over her eyes. She couldn't bear the sight. Unfortunately, six-year-olds have no such compunction. I stared long and hard, sick and trembling, yet entranced.

From the shoulders up, Delia was no longer recognizable as a human being. Her throat had been shredded and her jaw ripped away. Most of her hair and scalp were gone. There were long, bloody furrows in the creamy skin of her arms and legs. The organdy pinafore in which Fiona had dressed her that morning was clotted with blood, and the blood was still coming. Some of the walls were even spattered with it where the animal, whatever it was, had worried her in its frenzy. Her fists and heels banged jerkily against the floor. Our pet dog, Freddy, lay beside her, also bloody, but quite limp. Freddy's neck was broken.

I remember slowly raising my head—I must have been in shock by then—and meeting the bottomless gaze of the glass cat that sat on the hearth. Our father, a professor of art history, was very proud of this sculpture, for reasons I did not understand until many years later. I only knew it was valuable and we were not allowed to touch it. A chaotic feline travesty, it was not the sort of thing you would want to touch anyway. Though basically catlike in shape, it bristled with transparent threads and shards. There was something at once wild and vaguely human about its face. I had never liked it much, and Delia had always been downright frightened of it. On this day, as I looked up from my little sister's ruins, the cat seemed to glare at me with bright, terrifying satisfaction.

I had experienced, a year before, the thing every child fears most: the death of my mother. It had given me a kind of desperate strength, for I thought, at the tender age of six, that I had survived the worst life had to offer. Now, as I returned the mad stare of the glass cat, it came to me that I was wrong. The world was a much more evil place than I had ever imagined, and nothing would ever be the same again.

Delia died officially in the hospital a short time later. After a cursory investigation, the police laid the blame on Freddy. I still have the newspaper clipping, yellow now, and held together with even yellower cellophane tape. "The family dog lay dead near the victim, blood smearing its muzzle and forepaws. Sergeant Morton theorizes that the dog, a pit bull terrier and member of a breed specifically developed for vicious fighting, turned killer and attacked its tragic young owner. He also suggests that the child, during the death struggle, flung the murderous beast away with enough strength to break its neck."

Even I, a little girl, knew that this "theory" was lame; the neck of a pit bull is an almost impossible thing to break, even by a large, determined man. And Freddy, in spite of his breeding, had always been gentle, even protective, with us. Simply stated, the police were mystified, and this was the closest thing to a rational explanation they could produce. As far as they were concerned, that was the end of the matter. In fact, it had only just begun.

I was shipped off to my aunt Josie's house for several months. What Father did during this time I never knew, though I now suspect he spent those months in a sanitarium. In the course of a year, he had lost first his wife and then his daughter. Delia's death alone was the kind of outrage that might permanently have unhinged a lesser man. But a child has no way of knowing such things. I was bitterly angry at him for going away. Aunt Josie, though kind and good-hearted, was a virtual stranger to me, and I felt deserted. I had nightmares in which the glass cat slunk out of its place by the hearth and across the countryside. I would hear its hard claws ticking along the floor outside the room where I slept. At those times, half awake and screaming in the dark, no one could have comforted me except Father.

When he did return, the strain of his suffering showed. His face was thin and weary and his hair dusted with new gray, as if he had stood outside too long on a frosty night. On the afternoon of his arrival, he sat with me on Aunt Josie's sofa, stroking my cheek while I cuddled gladly, my anger at least temporarily forgotten in the joy of having him back.

His voice, when he spoke, was as tired as his face. "Well, my darling Amy, what do you suppose we should do now?"

"I don't know," I said. I assumed that, as always in the past, he had something entertaining in mind—that he would suggest it and then we would do it.

He sighed. "Shall we go home?"

I went practically rigid with fear. "Is the cat still there?"

Father looked at me, frowning slightly. "Do we have a cat?"

I nodded. "The big glass one."

He blinked, then made the connection. "Oh, the Chelichev, you mean? Well . . . I suppose it's still there. I hope so, in fact."

I clung to him, scrambling halfway up his shoulders in my panic. I could not manage to speak. All that came out of my mouth was an erratic series of whimpers.

"Sh, sh," said Father. I hid my face in the starched white cloth of his shirt and heard him whisper, as if to himself, "How can a glass cat frighten a child who's seen the things you've seen?"

"I hate him! He's glad Delia died. And now he wants to get *me*."

Father hugged me fiercely. "You'll never see him again.

I promise you," he said. And it was true, at least as long as he lived.

So the Chelichev *Cat in Glass* was packed away in a box and put into storage with the rest of our furnishings. Father sold the house, and we traveled for two years. When the horror had faded sufficiently, we returned home to begin a new life. Father went back to his professorship, and I to my studies at Chesly Girls' Day School. He bought a new house. The glass cat was not among the items he had sent up from storage. I did not ask him why. I was just as happy to forget about it, and forget it I did.

I neither saw the glass cat nor heard of it again until many years later. I was a grown woman by then, a school-teacher in a town far from the one in which I'd spent my childhood. I was married to a banker and had two lovely daughters and even a cat, which I finally permitted in spite of my abhorrence for them, because the girls begged so hard for one. I thought my life was settled, that it would progress smoothly toward a peaceful old age. But this was not to be. The glass cat had other plans.

The chain of events began with Father's death. It happened suddenly, on a snowy afternoon, as he graded papers in the tiny snug office he had always had on campus. A heart attack, they said. He was found seated at his desk, Erik Satie's Dadaist composition, "La Belle Excentrique," still spinning on the turntable of his record player.

I was not at all surprised to discover that he had left his affairs in some disarray. It's not that he had debts or was a gambler. Nothing so serious. It's just that order was slightly contrary to his nature. I remember once, as a very young woman, chiding him for the modest level of chaos he preferred in his life. "Really, Father," I said. "Can't you admire Dadaism without living it?" He laughed and admitted that he didn't seem able to.

As Father's only living relative, I inherited his house and other property, including his personal possessions. There were deeds to be transferred, insurance reports to be filed, bills and loans to be paid. He did have an attorney, an old school friend of his who helped me a great deal in organizing the storm of paperwork from a distance. The attorney also arranged for the sale of the house and hired someone to clean it out and ship the contents to us. In the course of the winter, a steady stream of cartons containing everything from scrapbooks to Chinese miniatures arrived at our doorstep. So I thought nothing of it when a large box labeled "fragile" was delivered one day by registered courier. There was a note from the attorney attached, explaining that he had just discovered it in a storage warehouse under Father's name and had had them ship it to me unopened.

It was a dismal February afternoon, a Friday. I had just come home from teaching. My husband, Stephen, had taken the girls to the mountains for a weekend of skiing, a sport I disliked. I had stayed behind and was looking forward to a couple of days of quiet solitude. The wind drove spittles of rain at the windows as I knelt on the floor of the front room and opened the box. I can't explain to you quite what I felt when I pulled away the packing paper and found myself face to face with the glass cat. Something akin to uncovering a nest of cockroaches in a drawer of sachet, I suppose. And that was swiftly followed by a horrid and minutely detailed mental recreation of Delia's death.

I swallowed my screams, struggling to replace them with something rational. "It's merely a glorified piece of glass." My voice bounced off the walls in the lonely house, hardly comforting.

I had an overpowering image of something inside me, something dark and featureless except for wide, white eyes and scrabbling claws. *Get us out of here!* it cried, and I obliged, seizing my coat from the closet hook and stumbling out into the wind.

I ran in the direction of town, slowing only when one of my shoes fell off and I realized how I must look. Soon, I found myself seated at a table in a diner, warming my hands in the steam from a cup of coffee, trying to convince myself that I was just being silly. I nursed the coffee as long as I could. It was dusk by the time I felt able to return home. There I found the glass cat, still waiting for me.

I turned on the radio for company and made a fire in the fireplace. Then I sat down before the box and finished unpacking it. The sculpture was as horrible as I remembered, truly ugly and disquieting. I might never have understood why Father kept it if he had not enclosed this letter of explanation, neatly handwritten on his college stationery:

To whom it may concern:

This box contains a sculpture, *Cat in Glass*, designed and executed by the late Alexander Chelichev. Because of Chelichev's standing as a noted forerunner of Dadaism, a historical account of *Cat's* genesis may be of interest to scholars.

I purchased *Cat* from the artist himself at his Zürich loft in December 1915, two months before the violent rampage which resulted in his confinement in a hospital for the criminally insane, and well before his artistic importance was widely recognized. (For the record, the asking price was forty-eight Swiss francs, plus a good meal with wine.) It is known that Chelichev had a wife and two children elsewhere in the city at that time, though he lived with them only sporadically. The following is the artist's statement about *Cat in Glass*, transcribed as accurately as possible from a conversation held with me during dinner.

"I have struggled with the devil all my life. He wants no rules. No order. His presence is everywhere in my work. I was beaten as a child, and when I became strong enough, I killed my father for it. I see you are skeptical, but it is true. Now I am a grown man and I find my father in myself. I have a wife and children, but I spend little time with them because I fear the father-devil in me. I do not beat my children. Instead I make this cat. Into the glass I have poured this madness of mine. Better there than in the eyes of my daughters."

It is my belief that *Cat in Glass* was Chelichev's last finished creation.

Sincerely,

Lawrence Waters

Professor of Art History

I closed the box, sealed it with the note inside, and spent the next two nights in a hotel, pacing the floor, sleeping little. The following Monday, Stephen took the cat to an art dealer for appraisal. He came home late that afternoon excited and full of news about the great Alexander Chelichev.

He made himself a gin and tonic as he expounded. "That glass cat is priceless, Amy. Did you realize? If your father had sold it, he'd have been independently wealthy. He never let on."

I was putting dinner on the table. The weekend had been a terrible strain. This had been a difficult day on top of it—snowy, and the children in my school class were wild with pent-up energy. So were our daughters, Eleanor and Rose, aged seven and four respectively. I could hear them quarreling in the playroom down the hall.

"Well, I'm glad to hear the horrid thing is worth something," I said. "Why don't we sell it and hire a maid?"

Stephen laughed as if I'd made an incredibly good joke. "A maid? You could hire a thousand maids for what that cat would bring at auction. It's a fascinating piece with an extraordinary history. You know, the value of something like this will increase with time. I think we'll do well to keep it awhile."

My fingers grew suddenly icy on the hot rim of the potato bowl. "I wasn't trying to be funny, Stephen. It's ugly and disgusting. If I could, I would make it disappear from the face of the Earth."

He raised his eyebrows. "What's this? Rebellion? Look, if you really want a maid, I'll get you one."

"That's not the point. I won't have the damned thing in my house."

"I'd rather you didn't swear, Amelia. The children might hear."

"I don't care if they do."

The whole thing degenerated from there. I tried to explain the cat's connection with Delia's death. But Stephen had stopped listening by then. He sulked through dinner. Eleanor and Rose argued over who got which spoonful of peas. And I struggled with a steadily growing sense of dread that seemed much too large for the facts of the matter.

When dinner was over, Stephen announced with exaggerated brightness, "Girls, we'd like your help in deciding an important question."

"Oh goody," said Rose.

"What is it?" said Eleanor.

"Please don't," I said. It was all I could do to keep from shouting.

Stephen flashed me the boyish grin with which he had originally won my heart. "Oh, come on. Try to look at it objectively. You're just sensitive about this because of an irrational notion from your childhood. Let the girls judge. If they like it, why not keep it?"

I should have ended it there. I should have insisted. Hindsight is always perfect, as they say. But inside me a little seed of doubt had sprouted. Stephen was always so logical and so right, especially about financial matters. Maybe he was right about this, too.

He had brought the thing home from the appraiser

without telling me. He was never above a little subterfuge if it got him his own way. Now he carried the carton in from the garage and unwrapped it in the middle of our warm, hardwood floor, with all the lights blazing. Nothing had changed. I found it as frightening as ever. I could feel cold sweat collecting on my forehead as I stared at it, all aglitter in a rainbow of refracted lamplight.

Eleanor was enthralled with it. She caught our real cat, a calico named Jelly, and held it up to the sculpture. "See, Jelly? You've got a handsome partner now." But Jelly twisted and hissed in Eleanor's arms until she let her go. Eleanor laughed and said Jelly was jealous.

Rose was almost as uncooperative as Jelly. She shrank away from the glass cat, peeking at it from between her father's knees. But Stephen would have none of that.

"Go on, Rose," he said. "It's just a kitty made of glass. Touch it and see." And he took her by the shoulders and pushed her gently toward it. She put out one hand, hesitantly, as she would have with a live cat who did not know her. I saw her finger touch a nodule of glass shards that might have been its nose. She drew back with a little yelp of pain. And that's how it began. So innocently.

"He bit me!" she cried.

"What happened?" said Stephen. "Did you break it?" He ran to the sculpture first, the brute, to make sure she hadn't damaged it.

She held her finger out to me. There was a tiny cut with a single drop of bright red blood oozing from it. "Mommy, it burns, it burns." She was no longer just crying. She was screaming.

We took her into the bathroom. Stephen held her while I washed the cut and pressed a cold cloth to it. The bleeding stopped in a moment, but still she screamed. Stephen grew angry. "What's this nonsense? It's a scratch. Just a scratch."

Rose jerked and kicked and bellowed. In Stephen's defense, I tell you now it was a terrifying sight, and he was never able to deal well with real fear, especially in himself. He always tried to mask it with anger. We had a neighbor who was a physician. "If you don't stop it, Rose, I'll call Doctor Pepperman. Is that what you want?" he said, as if Doctor Pepperman, a jolly septuagenarian, were anything but charming and gentle, as if threats were anything but asinine at such a time.

"For God's sake, get Pepperman! Can't you see something's terribly wrong?" I said.

And for once he listened to me. He grabbed Eleanor by the arm. "Come with me," he said and stomped across the yard through the snow without so much as a coat. I believe he only took Eleanor, also without a coat, because he was so unnerved that he didn't want to face the darkness alone.

Rose was still screaming when Dr. Pepperman arrived fresh from his dinner, specks of gravy clinging to his mustache. He examined Rose's finger and looked mildly puzzled when he had finished. "Can't see much wrong here. I'd say it's mostly a case of hysteria." He took a vial and a syringe from his small, brown case and gave Rose an injection, "to help settle her down," he said. It seemed to work. In a few minutes, Rose's screams had diminished to whimpers. Pepperman swabbed her finger with disinfectant and wrapped it loosely in gauze. "There, Rosie. Nothing like a bandage to make it feel better." He winked at us. "She should be fine in the morning. Take the gauze off as soon as she'll let you."

We put Rose to bed and sat with her till she fell asleep. Stephen unwrapped the gauze from her finger so the healing air could get to it. The cut was a bit red, but looked all right. Then we retired as well, reassured by the doctor, still mystified at Rose's reaction.

I awakened sometime after midnight. The house was muffled in the kind of silence brought by steady, soft snowfall. I thought I had heard a sound. Something odd. A scream? A groan? A snarl? Stephen still slept on the verge of a snore; whatever it was, it hadn't been loud enough to disturb him.

I crept out of bed and fumbled with my robe. There was a short flight of stairs between our room and the rooms where Rose and Eleanor slept. Eleanor, like her father, often snored at night, and I could hear her from the hallway now, probably deep in dreams. Rose's room was silent.

I went in and switched on the night-light. The bulb had very low wattage. I thought at first that the shadows were playing tricks on me. Rose's hand and arm looked black as a bruised banana. There was a peculiar odor in the air, like the smell of a butcher shop on a summer day. Heart galloping, I turned on the overhead light. Poor Rosie. She was so very still and clammy. And her arm was so very rotten.

They said Rose died from blood poisoning—a rare type most often associated with animal bites. I told them over and over again that it fit, that our child had indeed been bitten, by a cat, a most evil glass cat. Stephen was embarrassed. His own theory was that, far from blaming an apparently inanimate object, we ought to be suing Pepperman for malpractice. The doctors patted me sympathetically at first. Delusions brought on by grief, they said. It would pass. I would heal in time.

I made Stephen take the cat away. He said he would sell it, though in fact he lied to me. And we buried Rose. But I could not sleep. I paced the house each night, afraid to close my eyes because the cat was always there, glaring his satisfied glare, and waiting for new meat. And in the daytime, everything reminded me of Rosie. Fingerprints on the woodwork, the contents of the kitchen drawers, her favorite foods on the shelves of grocery stores. I could not teach. Every child had Rosie's face and Rosie's voice. Stephen and Eleanor were first kind, then gruff, then angry.

One morning, I could find no reason to get dressed or to move from my place on the sofa. Stephen shouted at me, told me I was ridiculous, asked me if I had forgotten that I still had a daughter left who needed me. But, you see, I no longer believed that I or anyone else could make any difference in the world. Stephen and Eleanor would get along with or without me. I didn't matter. There was no God of order and cause. Only chaos, cruelty, and whim.

When it was clear to Stephen that his dear wife Amy had turned from an asset into a liability, he sent me to an institution, far away from everyone, where I could safely be forgotten. In time, I grew to like it there. I had no responsibilities at all.

And if there was foulness and bedlam, it was no worse than the outside world.

There came a day, however, when they dressed me in a suit of new clothes and stood me outside the big glass and metal doors to wait; they didn't say for what. The air smelled good. It was springtime, and there were dandelions sprinkled like drops of fresh yellow paint across the lawn.

A car drove up and a pretty young woman got out and took me by the arm.

"Hello, Mother," she said as we drove off down the road. It was Eleanor, all grown up. For the first time since Rosie died, I wondered how long I had been away, and knew it must have been a very long while.

We drove a considerable distance, to a large suburban house, white, with a sprawling yard and a garage big enough for two cars. It was a mansion compared to the house in which Stephen and I had raised her. By way of making polite small talk, I asked if she was married, whether she had children. She climbed out of the car looking irritated. "Of course I'm married," she said. "You've met Jason. And you've seen pictures of Sarah and Elizabeth often enough." Of this I had no recollection.

She opened the gate in the picket fence, and we started up the neat, stone walkway. The front door opened a few inches, and small faces peered out. The door opened wider, and two little girls ran onto the porch.

"Hello," I said. "And who are you?"

The older one, giggling behind her hand, said, "Don't you know, Grandma? I'm Sarah."

The younger girl stayed silent, staring at me with frank curiosity.

"That's Elizabeth. She's afraid of you," said Sarah.

I bent and looked into Elizabeth's eyes. They were brown, and her hair was shining blond, like Rosie's. "No need to be afraid of me, my dear. I'm just a harmless old woman."

Elizabeth frowned. "Are you crazy?" she asked.

Sarah giggled behind her hand again, and Eleanor breathed loudly through her nose as if this impertinence was simply overwhelming.

I smiled. I liked Elizabeth. Liked her very much. "They say I am," I said, "and it may very well be true."

A tiny smile crossed her face. She stretched on her tiptoes and kissed my cheek, hardly more than the touch of a warm breeze, then turned and ran away. Sarah followed her, and I watched them go, my heart dancing and shivering. I had loved no one in a very long time. I missed it, but dreaded it, too. For I had loved Delia and Rosie, and they were both dead.

The first thing I saw when I entered the house was Chelichev's *Cat in Glass*, glaring evilly from a place of obvious honor on a low pedestal near the sofa. My stomach felt suddenly shrunken.

"Where did you get that?" I said.

Eleanor looked irritated again. "From Daddy, of course."

"Stephen promised me he would sell it!"

"Well, I guess he didn't, did he?"

Anger heightened my pulse. "Where is he? I want to speak to him immediately."

"Mother, don't be absurd. He's been dead for ten years."

I lowered myself into a chair. I was shaking by then, and I fancied I saw a half smile on the glass cat's cold jowls.

"Get me out of here," I said. A great weight crushed my lungs. I could barely breathe.

With a look, I must say, of genuine worry, Eleanor escorted me onto the porch and brought me a tumbler of ice water. "Better?" she asked.

I breathed deeply. "A little. Eleanor, don't you realize that monstrosity killed your sister, and mine as well?"

"That simply isn't true."

"But it is, it is! I'm telling you now, get rid of it if you care for the lives of your children."

Eleanor went pale, whether from rage or fear I could not tell. "It isn't yours. You're legally incompetent, and I'll thank you to stay out of my affairs as much as possible till you have a place of your own. I'll move you to an apartment as soon as I can find one."

"An apartment? But I can't . . . "

"Yes you can. You're as well as you're ever going to be, Mother. You only liked that hospital because it was easy. Well it costs a lot of money to keep you there, and we can't afford it anymore. You're just going to have to straighten up and start behaving like a human being again."

By then I was very close to tears, and very confused as well. Only one thing was clear to me, and that was the true nature of the glass cat. I said, in as steady a voice as I could muster, "Listen to me. That cat was made out of madness. It's evil. If you have a single ounce of brains, you'll put it up for auction this very afternoon."

"So I can get enough money to send you back to the hospital, I suppose? Well I won't do it. That sculpture is priceless. The longer we keep it, the more it's worth."

She had Stephen's financial mind. I would never sway her, and I knew it. I wept in despair, hiding my face in my hands. I was thinking of Elizabeth. The sweet, soft skin of her little arms, the flame in her cheeks, the power of that small kiss. Human beings are such frail works of art, their lives so precarious, and here I was again, my wayward heart gone out to one of them. But the road back to the safety of isolation lay in ruins. The only way out was through.

Jason came home at dinnertime, and we ate a nice meal, seated around the sleek rosewood table in the dining room. He was kind, actually far kinder than Eleanor. He asked the children about their day and listened carefully while they replied. As did I, enraptured by their pink perfection, distraught at the memory of how imperfect a child's flesh can become. He did not interrupt. He did not demand. When Eleanor refused to give me coffee—she said she was afraid it would get me "hyped up"—he admonished her and poured me a cup himself. We talked about my father, whom he knew by reputation, and about art and the cities of Europe. All the while, I felt in my bones the baleful gaze of the *Cat in Glass,* burning like the coldest ice through walls and furniture as if they did not exist.

Eleanor made up a cot for me in the guest room. She didn't want me to sleep in the bed and she wouldn't tell me why. But I overheard Jason arguing with her about it. "What's wrong with the bed?" he said.

"She's mentally ill," said Eleanor. She was whispering, but loudly. "Heaven only knows what filthy habits she's picked up. I won't risk her soiling a perfectly good mattress. If she does well on the cot for a few nights, then we can consider moving her to the bed."

They thought I was in the bathroom, performing whatever unspeakable acts it is that mentally ill people perform in places like that, I suppose. But they were wrong. I was sneaking past their door, on my way to the garage. Jason must have been quite a handyman in his spare time. I found a large selection of hammers on the wall, including an excellent short-handled sledge. I hid it under my bedding. They never even noticed.

The children came in and kissed me good-night in a surreal reversal of roles. I lay in the dark on my cot for a long time, thinking of them, especially of Elizabeth, the youngest and weakest, who would naturally be the most likely target of an animal's attack. I dozed, dreaming sometimes of a smiling Elizabeth-Rose-Delia, sifting snow, wading through drifts; sometimes of the glass cat, its fierce eyes smoldering, crystalline tongue brushing crystalline jaws. The night was well along when the dreams crashed down like broken mirrors into silence.

The house was quiet except for those ticks and thumps all houses make as they cool in the darkness. I got up and slid the hammer out from under the bedding, not even sure what I was going to do with it, knowing only that the time had come to act.

I crept out to the front room, where the cat sat waiting, as I knew it must. Moonlight gleamed in the chaos of its glass fur. I could feel its power, almost see it, a shimmering red aura the length of its malformed spine. The thing was moving, slowly, slowly, smiling now, oh yes, a real smile. I could smell its rotten breath.

For an instant, I was frozen. Then I remembered the hammer, Jason's lovely short-handled sledge. And I raised it over my head and brought it down in the first crashing blow.

The sound was wonderful. Better than cymbals, better even than holy trumpets. I was trembling all over, but I went on and on in an agony of satisfaction while glass fell like moonlit rain. There were screams. "Grandma, stop! Stop!" I swung the hammer back in the first part of another arc, heard something like the thunk of a fallen ripe melon, swung it down on the cat again. I couldn't see anymore. It came to me that there was glass in my eyes and blood in my mouth. But none of that mattered, a small price to pay for the long overdue demise of Chelichev's *Cat in Glass*.

So you see how I have come to this, not without many sacrifices along the way. And now the last of all: The sockets where my eyes used to be are infected. They stink. Blood poisoning, I'm sure.

I wouldn't expect Eleanor to forgive me for ruining her prime investment. But I hoped Jason might bring the children a time or two anyway. No word except for the delivery of a single rose yesterday. The matron said it was white and held it up for me to sniff, and she read me the card that came with it. "Elizabeth was a great one for forgiving. She would have wanted you to have this. Sleep well, Jason."

Which puzzled me.

"You don't even know what you've done, do you?" said the matron.

"I destroyed a valuable work of art," said I.

But she made no reply.

LUNCH AT ETIENNE'S

Marion Cumberly sorted through her winter coats, a bother, but it had to be done. July or not, she could see her breath. A fragile layer of ice had formed on all the puddles, indoors and out, and there was even snow of a sort, grayish and not very wet. The weather seemed to be out of order lately. She sighed. If the phone were working, she would have called the president of the American Meteorological Association, an old school chum of her husband's, to complain directly. She wished Mrs. Halprin, the housekeeper, would come to work again so she could tell her about the phone and get it repaired properly. Mrs. Halprin was a veritable sorceress when it came to dealing with service people. But Mrs. Halprin seemed to have disappeared.

Marion slapped irritably at the coats. Puffs of whitish powder rose from them. The closet doors had fallen off, so the coats, like everything else, had gotten covered with dust. The question was, which one should she wear to Chez Etienne for her luncheon date with Irene Rutledge. She had two furs—a mink and a Russian sable. The sable was extremely warm. She reached for it, then hesitated, her small hand hovering over the silky fur. Now that she thought of it, the sable wouldn't do. Chez Etienne was an elegant place, but unassuming. She would be overdressed, and everyone would stare at her as she came through the door. It was bad enough having to bring little Nicky along. At a place like Chez Etienne, a woman in the company of a two-year-old would be a spectacle, even without a sable coat.

Immediately, she felt ashamed of herself for having thought such a thing. After all, it was hardly Nicky's fault that his babysitter had never arrived. Marion smiled as she thought of her little son's wide, blue eyes and curly hair, so pale it was almost white. Everyone who saw him declared that he was the brightest, most beautiful child they had ever seen. The babysitter, an older woman, adored him— brought him small gifts and candy whenever she came, which was supposed to be three times a week: Mondays, Wednesdays, and Fridays. On Wednesdays, she came an hour earlier than usual so Marion could leave for her weekly lunch date with Irene. But here it was, almost noon, and almost certainly Wednesday. Marion was late for her lunch, and the sitter still had not arrived. She had missed last week's lunch at Etienne's—she couldn't quite remember why—and it would be unthinkably embarrassing to miss it yet again. There was nothing for it but to take Nicky with her to the restaurant.

She flicked through her coats one last time and nodded as she made up her mind. There was always the blue velvet— so versatile. She lifted it carefully from the hanger, gave it three good smacks to get the worst of the dust, then pulled it on over the silk blouse and three wool sweaters she was already wearing.

"Time to go, Nicky," she called as she threaded her way toward the nursery.

One had to be careful. There were several holes in the ceiling, and two in the floor. Broken glass littered the rugs. The windows all were shattered. She had asked the handy-man about fixing them when she had run into him outside on the walk two days ago. But he had only bared his teeth at her and mumbled in a breathless sort of way, "The hell with your windows, you bitch!"

She had never approved of people who cursed.

Nicky was sitting in his crib, right where she had left him, looking like a little man in his short pants and blazer. She held her hands out toward him. "All ready to go, pummy cake?"

He glared at her.

"Don't you want to come with Mommy, Nicky pie?"

He remained stubbornly motionless in the corner of his crib. It wasn't like him. He usually beamed and chortled at the prospect of going places. Marion sighed once more.

Maybe he wasn't feeling well. She felt a little under the weather herself—nothing major, a few stomach troubles and general tiredness. Still, even small ailments could make a person cranky, especially a baby.

On the other hand, maybe it was something simpler. Maybe Nicky missed his father. Gerald, a financial analyst in the city thirty miles away, traveled a great deal in his work. He hadn't been home in some time. She couldn't remember his mentioning it, but she assumed he was gone on a business trip.

"Never mind, Nicky, dear. Daddy will be home soon," she said as she reached down and picked him up.

Marion became aware of an unpleasant odor in the air and discreetly opened the waistband of Nicky's pants to check his diaper. Clean and dry, so that couldn't be it. She had noticed the odor several times lately and wished she could call the pediatrician about it. But of course, that wasn't possible until the phone was repaired.

Marion tottered downstairs with Nicky balanced on her hip, trying not to rely too much on the banister, which had come loose. She considered setting Nicky down and letting him scramble to the bottom by himself, but he wasn't very good at stairs yet. And besides, in a mood like this, he would probably just sit down, cross his little arms, and refuse to budge anyway.

When she reached the entryway, she laid her hand on the front door latch, then realized her mistake and laughed aloud at her own silliness. The front entrance was no use because it was blocked by a heap of broken masonry—

another thing the handyman had refused to clean up. Fortunately, the house was lovely and old, built long before the Bauhaus school had transformed architecture into an array of featureless walls and sterile lines. It possessed all the amenities, including a wondrous number of doors, any of which could be used instead of the front entrance.

She stepped gingerly over the chandelier and several icy puddles that had accumulated from drips in the ceiling. The plumbing as well as the phones seemed badly out of order. She made her way toward the kitchen, thinking how glad she was that at least she didn't have to rely on the broken pipes for drinking. She and Gerald always kept a large supply of bottled spring water on hand.

On her way to the kitchen door, she stopped in front of the pantry, pressing the tip of one finger to her cheek as she considered a new complication. She and Irene enjoyed Chez Etienne so much because Etienne provided excellent food with impeccable service. But things were in such a turmoil lately that even Etienne might find his resources strained.

Marion set Nicky on the drainboard and began rummaging through one of the kitchen drawers. After a time, she located some matches, lit a candle, and held it up in the dark little pantry. She hesitated only a moment before pulling a can of vichyssoise and a jar of artichoke hearts from the shelf. She loaded them into her coat pockets along with the matches and a can opener, muttering to herself. Gerald wouldn't approve. He would say she was too soft on service people, and she knew it was true, but she couldn't help feeling kindly toward Etienne after so many years of wonderful Wednesday lunches in his establishment.

"Here we go, Nicky," she said. And she opened the back door.

The gray snow was still falling, and it was even colder outside than inside. A gust of raw wind stung her cheeks.

"Oh, poor Nicky, dear!" she cried, suddenly remembering that she hadn't been able to find his coat, and his legs were bare. She opened her own coat, pressed him close, and wrapped it around him as well as she could, wishing fiercely that she hadn't been so vain, that she had worn the warm Russian sable instead of the velvet.

She blinked at the sun, nothing more than a light gray spot in the heavy gray sky, and tried hard to suppress a quite involuntary shudder. "There are times," her mother had always said, "when a person of good breeding must overlook conditions, behave with good humor, and rise to the occasion." She turned as smartly as she could on the buckled sidewalk and started down the street toward Etienne's, stepping over a downed power pole and making a wide detour around the first heap of rubble.

She waved as she passed the Sutherlands' house. The front wall had fallen down, and there was Mrs. Sutherland, sitting on the sofa, rocking back and forth with a large bundle in her arms. Something gray and brown and tattered. Marion couldn't quite tell what it was.

"Halloo, Mrs. Sutherland," she called. "How's little Alex these days?"

Mrs. Sutherland stopped rocking, stared at her, and said nothing, absolutely nothing. Her face went stiff as wood. She wasn't looking well.

"I say, how's Alex doing?" Marion repeated.

Just as if Marion weren't there at all, Mrs. Sutherland started rocking again.

Marion frowned and continued down the street, thinking that Mrs. Sutherland, who seemed of good quality otherwise, must have a serious deficiency in her upbringing. Obviously, no one had ever taught her about rising to the occasion.

She passed several other people on her way and smiled and nodded at each one, but no one smiled in return. In fact, one fellow, wrapped up in a soiled wool overcoat with the lapels pulled together as if his life depended on it, started weeping and ran away from her. By the time she reached Etienne's, she felt rather out of sorts herself.

The front doors at Chez Etienne, made of heavy oak with weathered brass fittings, were stuck. Marion had to perch Nicky on a tilted bus stop bench while she cleared away a tangle of rubbish and tugged the doors open. She grabbed Nicky up and went inside. She could hardly see anything. There was only one window, which, Etienne had once explained to her, made for a cozier atmosphere. Remembering the matches in her pocket, she lit several of the candles that always stood in crystal holders on the tables.

As the light in the room grew to a warm glow, Marion found her way to the quiet table in the rear where she and

Irene usually sat. Some plaster from the ceiling had come down, and the chairs were quite dusty. While she was wiping them off with her handkerchief, she spied Irene, sitting against the wall in the corner.

"Irene! How wonderful to see you. I was afraid you might not make it, with everything in such a state."

Irene had a surprised look on her face. Her hat, a Garbo-style felt, was tipped at a jaunty angle on her head, and powdered plaster frosted the shoulders of her jacket.

Marion settled Nicky in a chair and scooted him up to the table. Then she rushed over to Irene. "Here. Let me help you up. Really, it's so wonderful to see you," she said, and grabbed Irene under the arms.

It was a little awkward getting her into a chair, but Marion managed. As she stopped to catch her breath, she noticed the unpleasant odor again. She sniffed the air, wondering if it was Nicky. But this time, the odor was definitely coming from Irene. She shrugged it off. It wasn't important, after all, and at any rate, it wasn't the sort of thing one mentioned in public.

Neither Etienne nor any of the waiters seemed to be about, so she fished the vichyssoise and artichoke hearts from her coat pockets. "I've come prepared!" she said, and laughed gaily. "Isn't it terrible, the mess everything's in?"

Irene said nothing. Perhaps she wasn't feeling very talkative.

"Really, I've been so worried that you'd be angry at me for missing last Wednesday. But the phones are impossible. I couldn't call. So I just had to trust your good nature. You don't mind it that I brought Nicky, do you? He's being so good. I'm afraid his sitter didn't come today. Really, you're not angry, are you?"

Still, Irene said nothing. Marion felt suddenly breathless and warm, as if she might burst into tears any moment. How odd. There was nothing to cry about, after all. She glanced at the wavering shadows the candles cast on the walls and shut her eyes against an inexplicable flood of panic.

"Here. Here," she said. "There's not enough light, don't you think?" And she hurried around to the other tables, gathering up all the candles she could find. She set them in front of Irene and lit each one carefully.

Still, Irene did not speak.

It was then that Marion saw the scene in the mirror. The entire north wall of Chez Etienne was lined with mirror glass; it made the room seem larger, Etienne had told them once, passing the time of day while a waiter twisted the pepper mill over their salads. Now, amid chaos and destruction, the mirror remained perversely intact. Reflected in it, Marion saw first a brilliant cluster of candle flames in the center of a table. She didn't recognize the woman who stood by the table, a filthy hag who regarded her with a faint smile and bright, demented eyes—a bag lady, she thought, who must have wandered away from her home in the city subway tunnels. Beside her sat two people who, Marion slowly realized, were actually corpses in varying degrees of decomposition. One was that of a small child, the other that of a lady who had once been stylishly dressed.

Marion felt a sudden rush of warmth and pity for the bag lady. "Oh, my dear," she said, leaning forward.

"Oh, my dear," said the woman in the mirror, leaning forward at precisely the same moment.

Marion blinked and shuddered. A tiny whimper escaped from her throat. Not wanting to, not wanting to at all, Marion began to remember in vivid detail exactly why she had missed last week's lunch at Etienne's.

"No," she cried, staring into Etienne's mirror. "No, no, no!"

Marion Cumberly, who had never done such a thing in her life, picked up a chair and threw it into the mirror. Shards of glass flew sparkling into the air, and in their place appeared a wall of blessed, empty shadow.

Marion smiled. "Shall we have some vichyssoise, Irene, dear?" she said. "I'm not sure whether Nicky will like it. He's never tried it before."

And with a flourish, she produced the can opener from the pocket of her coat.

THE SAILOR'S BARGAIN

I am whimpering in my sleep again. Across the abyss between our beds, I hear my friend Mary Fairfax calling my name.

"Electra. Electra! Wake up."

But I can't seem to separate her voice from the cobweb fabric of the dream. Neither can I separate the roar of the wind from the roar of my own blood, or tell which is real and which imagined.

"Wake up!"

Fairfax crosses the dark room, grabs my shoulders.

In my dream, I kneel on the rain-swept deck of a wooden ship, a ship with many sails, huge and dark. Waves crash over the bow, and the masts groan as if they are about to splinter. In my dream, the wind shakes me until my teeth clack. It tears at me, and it laughs, and it says, *A bargain is a bargain, part and parcel.*

Then I realize that the bow of the ship is really the chapel of the orphanage in San Francisco where I grew up. I am taking part in the celebration of some skewed Mass. A canticle response rises to my lips. It is part of no prayer I have ever heard. I do not know where it came from. *My days are swifter than a weaver's shuttle, and are spent without hope. O remember that my life is wind.*

At once, the chaos of the dream falls away, a black mirror shattered by words, and I am sitting up, staring into Fairfax's face. Dim light from a street lamp seeps through the window. In it I can see the disheveled spikes of her hair, like a fiery halo, which I have envied since we were children, and the wrinkled impression her pillow has left across one of her cheeks. The orphanage and the chapel and the ship have disappeared. It has happened just the same way almost every night for two months.

"Shit," says Fairfax. "I can't take anymore of this. Either get some help, or I'm moving out."

I press the sheets against my forehead to soak away the dream sweat. I look around the room. It takes me a moment to realize that I'm not seeing the adobe walls of the dormitory at Our Lady of the Harbor. It's been almost two years since Fairfax and I left the Catholic orphanage. Now we live on the campus at Las Piedras University, in a "temporary dorm"—really just a trailer with several sleeping cubicles and a big bathroom.

Outside I hear the night wind rushing from the land to the sea, prowling around beaverboard corners, scrabbling at the cheap window frames. This little box of a shelter feels like paper compared to Our Lady of the Harbor, with its thick walls, oak beams, and heavy, nail-studded doors.

"I don't want any help," I say. "I've made up my mind this dream is never coming back again."

But Fairfax knows me too well.

She sighs and switches on my chipped bedside lamp. In its comforting yellow glow, our room is a perfect illustration of the differences between us. My side is cluttered with treasures I have gathered at random from secondhand stores and flea markets, while hers is stark and clean as a monk's cell. I buy wobbly tables, hats with holes in them, and boxes full of crystals and buttons. Fairfax prefers modern European prints and slim watches with no numbers on their faces.

She sits beside me on the bed, naked except for a pair of kelly green satin bikinis and a thin gold necklace. She refuses to wear nightclothes. They get tangled around her like ropes in the night, she says, and they're good for nothing.

She hugs herself in the cool night air. Her skin is covered with freckles and goose bumps. "Nobody, not even you, can just decide not to have a dream. You know as well as I do it'll be back again. This isn't normal, Electra. Something's wrong."

She looks down at the linoleum floor, looks up again, her chin held very high. "I think I really mean it. You and your nightmares are driving me crazy. If you don't talk to somebody about this, I'm moving out."

She turns off the light. I listen to the slap of her feet on the floor as she walks back to her bed. I pull the covers up and stare out the window at the thrashing treetops. In her own way, she is just trying to help.

The next morning, a Tuesday, Fairfax is sitting in her bathrobe playing her cello when I leave our room. I wave good-bye, as usual; she nods vaguely, as usual, without taking her eyes from the music.

I have an early class on Tuesdays, number theory, the only course I am taking this quarter. In June, when the summer term opened, the elegance and purity of number theory delighted me—made the world seem acute, well formed, and larger than humankind. But now it is August. For two months, dreams of wind and ships have robbed me of sleep. Often, the concepts our professor introduces make no sense to me, and sometimes proofs that would have seemed obvious before escape me.

This morning, just as I expect, I doze through the class. When the hour is over, the professor takes me aside. "Electra, I regard you as one of our most promising mathematics majors. But lately I've noticed a certain . . . shall we say . . . lack of concentration. Is anything wrong?"

"No. No, nothing at all," I say, staring at my feet. Some men, most men in fact, make me nervous. In front of this male teacher, I'm an even more inept liar than usual.

He frowns and rubs his neck.

"Sorry," I mumble. "I'm late. I really have to be going."

I hurry out of the classroom toward the cafeteria, where I usually eat breakfast after class. On my way, I pass the campus chapel and hesitate there, trying to compose my rattled nerves. In its distant beginnings, Las Piedras was a Catholic school. Now it is secular, but the chapel remains for those who wish to use it. I have been inside it often for Mass.

I stop on the terrazzo plaza in front to look up at the gilt mosaic on the chapel's facade, of Christ walking on the water after he has calmed the storm. For no reason at all, goose flesh rises on my arms. It is a cloudless, brilliant day, and a warm breeze drifts inland from the ocean, heavy with the smell of seaweed. It blows my hair across my eyes so that all the world becomes the color of sand.

In that moment, everything reels and folds, and I am plunged into my nightmare without warning. This time, I seem to be looking down on the black ship from midair. It is the same ship, wooden, with seven or eight square sails. Towering waves ram her broadside, and she heels and screams. I gasp for air, afraid that I will die if she dies. I have had the dream many times before but never like this, wide awake, in the middle of a daily routine. I try to claw my way back to the solid reality of the plaza and the glittering mosaic.

But when I come to myself, I am not on the plaza as I expect to be. I am lying prone on a broad stairway with my arms wrapped around a wooden post—a communion rail, I slowly realize. I look up. I recognize the shape of the vaulted arches above my head and the stained glass depictions of the stations of the cross. I am inside the chapel.

I stumble to my feet, dizzy and disoriented. Beyond the rail, the altar stands bare. The altar cloth lies on the floor beneath it, a heap of embroidered laundry. A huge Bible lies beside it, stricken from its stand, pages bent and torn, spine broken. I turn and face the pews. Missals lie scattered in the aisles. Smoke rises in ghostly ribbons from the wicks of a dozen extinguished votive candles.

My days are swifter than a weaver's shuttle, and are spent without hope. O remember that my life is wind. The words echo inside my skull.

A cold draft moans through the nave, ruffling the pages of the scattered missals; or is it someone laughing? The hair on the back of my neck stands up. My heart quickens, a hundred beats a minute, a hundred and ten, two every second. I bolt from the chapel, through the double doors, and into the sunlight.

I am halfway across the quad before I can overcome my panic enough to stop running. I pant and glance around to make sure no one has seen my windmilling flight. After a moment, I force myself to walk slowly, deliberately toward the cafeteria, repeating in a low whisper, "I am tired. I must have imagined it all. I am tired . . ."

When I reach the cafeteria, I buy a sugar doughnut and black coffee. While I stand in line at the cash register, a hundred wild thoughts jostle against each other in my brain, trying to dislodge my careful concentration on the mundane matters of napkins and correct change.

It doesn't matter what I tell myself. I know what I saw was real. The chapel looked as if a gale had been set loose inside it. It looked as if my nightmare had come to life. But this is childish nonsense, and I am not a child anymore. I am twenty years old, twenty-one in November—too old to be frightened by dreams, especially dreams like these. I have never been on a ship in my life. And as for the wind, I have always loved being out in it—flying kites, or even just walking, wrapped up in a snug coat and hat. I cannot recall any reason to fear either wind or ships.

But while I count out two quarters, a dime, two nickels, and place them in the cashier's hand, the great fact of my life runs its bony fingers up my spine, as it has countless times before. I will never be an entirely known quantity to anyone, even to myself. I may never know where the nightmare came from. I am no ordinary person. I am not even an ordinary orphan. I am, in fact, a foundling.

I sit down at one of the tables outside and watch analytically while tears splash into my steaming coffee. I can't bring myself to look up and see who is pulling out the chair across from me.

"Hey."

It is Fairfax. She places the palm of her hand on my forehead and pushes gently, until my face is tilted up toward hers.

"What's the matter?" she says.

I shake my head. I'm not sure I can talk yet, not even to Fairfax. But an instant later, the words come out in an unexpected rush.

"I . . . I was walking across the plaza. I had the dream." My voice cracks and I stop, feeling helpless.

Fairfax wrinkles her forehead. Is it concern or incredulity? "About the wind? In the middle of the day?"

I nod miserably. "I had the dream and when I woke up I was inside the chapel. It was a mess. Fairfax, the wind had been blowing inside. It blew out the candles. It tore the cloth off the altar. What am I going to do?"

She smiles. It *is* incredulity. "Naw," she says. "It's just a dream. How could a dream do that? Come on, now. You know you were imagining things."

"But I wasn't. You don't know what it was like. I couldn't have imagined it."

Fairfax presses her lips into a thin, determined line and takes me by the arm. "All right. Show me," she says.

Tension arcs between us as we walk silently back toward the chapel. When we reach it, Fairfax pulls open the big wooden doors, and we peer into the nave. Even before my eyes adjust to the dim light, I know I was right. The chapel is alive with voices—high, angry, frightened. "You're certain you didn't see anyone? Who would do such a thing?"

Fairfax's eyes grow huge as she surveys the damage. She grabs my arm and hustles me back across the plaza to a bench beneath a palm tree. "Electra, I think we should talk," she says.

"I told you," I say. "It really happened."

She shakes her head violently. "This couldn't possibly have any connection with your dream. Be rational. There's got to be some other explanation."

"No. It has something to do with me. I know it."

"Don't be crazy. It's just a coincidence. Maybe it's vandals. Or somebody playing a practical joke."

"No. It's me. The wind is trying to get me."

"Fine. If that's really what you think, then you should go see a doctor." She almost shouts it.

"A doctor can't help me!"

Fairfax closes her eyes and silently mouths the numbers one to twenty. Her temper is quick and terrible. Sometimes even the counting doesn't keep it from getting out of control.

When she reaches twenty-one, she gets up, still red-faced, and slings her book bag over her shoulder. "I'm late for my class," she says, biting the words off and spitting them out. She spins and stalks off across the plaza, leaving me alone beneath the tree.

I don't see her again till after dinner, when she shows up at the trailer dorm with a familiar grin on her face. I have seen this grin before—the broad one that means she is pleased with herself and bursting to tell me about it.

"Sorry about this morning," I say. I am sitting cross-legged on my bed, working proofs and watching a talk show on my television, an old black-and-white with all the dials missing.

She flounces down beside me. "Oh, forget about that. I've got a great plan."

I look at her warily. Her last great plan was for me to sell my collection of comic books and put the money down on a used Alfa Romeo.

"I've spent the whole day getting all the details worked out. Look, this flimsy trailer is a terrible place for anybody who's having nightmares about the wind. I think we should both get out of here."

I frown. She is so impulsive. "Where would we go?"

Fairfax opens her book pack and pulls out a folded sheet of binder paper with a message neatly printed on it in soft pencil. "Room and board, reasonable rates. Dr. and Mrs. Axelrod Desmond, 713 Melville Street, 322-1732."

"What's this?"

"You know my physics instructor, Tony DiMarini?"

I nod. She has mentioned him once or twice, mostly in connection with his niceness. Fairfax, a music major, is in the midst of struggling through a required physics course. She told me when she signed up for it that she thought summer would be the best time to take it because instructors have more free time to work with students then.

"Well, I ran into him after class today," she says. "He mentioned that there are a couple of rooms open at the place where he lives. It's an old house near campus. Interested?"

I chew on my pencil eraser. The whole thing sounds to me like some kind of ploy on DiMarini's part.

"It belongs to a retired English professor and his wife. They rent out the rooms on the top story for practically nothing, to any students who are willing to help with chores and yard work."

"Sounds suspicious," I say. "It's probably a real dump or something. Either that or the yard work's a full-time job."

Fairfax breathes loudly through her nose. "Electra! Don't be that way. I wouldn't get you into anything like that. It's a wonderful place."

I squint at her, suddenly aware that she's holding something back. "How do you know it's a wonderful place?"

"Look . . . uh . . . I telephoned Mrs. Desmond. I went over to see it this afternoon. Oh, Electra, you'll love it! It's huge. It's made of solid stone. And the Desmonds are terrific. They didn't want to take the deposit at first, not till they'd met you . . ." Her voice trails off. "Uh-oh," she says. She touches her lips with her fingertips.

"You mean you *rented* it? Without even asking me?"

"I knew you'd love it, I just knew it, and if I didn't take it right then, somebody else would. Tony had to put in a good word for us, as it was. Oh, Electra, won't you at least try it for a while?"

Fairfax is glowing with excitement. Her eyes shine like the sun on a green sea. At times like these, she is practically irresistible. I don't suppose I can really blame DiMarini for trying to get closer to her.

I look at the address again, trying to be critical. 713 Melville Street. In spite of myself, I picture a high, bright room with a view. 713. Seven for good luck, thirteen for bad. I think of the way our dingy, cramped trailer shudders in the least breath of wind. I really do hate it. Fairfax is right. It is a very bad place for someone with dreams like mine.

"Oh all right," I say at last.

Fairfax and I spend the next morning at the university housing office, getting out of our dorm arrangement. In the afternoon, we make the short trek to Melville Street, up a hill north of campus. True to Fairfax's description, number 713 is a three-story house with thick fieldstone walls and a broad porch. An ancient willow tree guards the front yard, its roots buckling the sidewalk into tilted plates. We walk up the steps and rap on the heavy front door but get no answer.

"I guess the Desmonds aren't home, but trust me," says Fairfax. "You'll love it."

I nod. "Probably right," I say, with a faint sense of discomfort. I don't like being pushed into such a big change. But as far as I can tell, Fairfax has been completely truthful about the house. It looks huge, sturdy, and inviting. Besides, now that the paperwork with the housing office is finished, it will be easier to move than to stay in the dormitory.

The following Saturday, Fairfax and I collect cardboard cartons from supermarket trash bins and pack our belongings in them. She fills six boxes; I fill fifteen, even after I have thrown away everything I can bear to part with. I wish possessions were not so important to me. Sometimes I suspect myself of trying to build a past with them, article by article.

Fairfax sits on the floor, tossing items from my "must keep" pile into the open cartons, stopping now and then to examine something that catches her interest. She tries on a sequined black glove, crooks her little finger as if she were drinking tea, and laughs.

"Where's the mate to this?" she asks.

"As far as I know, it's never had one," I reply.

She opens an old cigar box and holds up one of the many sand dollars she finds inside it. "I remember the day we gathered these!" she says. "On that beach up north where Sister Michael and Sister Mary Rose used to take us camping." She half smiles and tilts her head. "We were just little girls. You've saved them all these years?"

I smile and nod. Though I'll never really know, I imagine that Fairfax and I are a lot like blood relatives.

Tony DiMarini has offered to help us move. I've been thinking about him off and on, in a cranky and distrustful way. I imagine him as a handsome young professor in his thirties, neatly attired in an Oxford-cloth shirt with the sleeves rolled up just so, like the men in aftershave ads. Someone suave and unscrupulous who is probably after the body of every pretty redhead on campus.

It is late afternoon when he taps on our open door. He clears his throat, says, "Hi, is this the right place?" and trips over something invisible as he walks into our room. While Fairfax and I help him up, my rakish image of him dissolves into one of herons, mostly their legs, knobby and impossibly fragile. He has frizzy blond hair, and there are holes in the seat of his jeans, through which I catch a glimpse of plaid boxer shorts. The collar of his rumpled shirt is buttoned, and his Adam's apple jumps up and down above it like a skinny, hairless mouse every time he speaks. I like him almost immediately, perhaps because he is not at all what I expected. If he is attracted to Fairfax, he will have to work hard to get her.

Tony's car is a convertible with a dangling front bumper and an engine that sounds like a freight train. "Nineteen sixty-four Bonneville. They don't make them like this any-more," he says, proudly tapping the hood. The car is so huge that all twenty-one of our cartons fit easily into the back-seat and the trunk. There is plenty of room for the three of us, and Fairfax's cello, on the bench seat in front.

When we reach the new house, Lavinia Desmond, tiny, platinum-haired, and dressed in summer woolens, greets us at the door.

"Roddy. Roddy!" she calls, as she leads us through the vestibule. "Mary Fairfax and her friend have arrived."

Roddy pokes his head around a corner, plucks a briar pipe from his purplish lips, and waves it gleefully. "Hello, Mary." He gazes in my direction and lifts a bushy eyebrow. "And you must be . . . ?" he says.

"Electra Thorpe."

"Of course. Lovely, lovely," he cries, clasping my hand in his.

"I've already listed the house rules for Mary, my dear," says Lavinia as she leads us up the polished hardwood stairs. "But for your benefit I'll mention them again. No parakeets. I can't stand cleaning the little doo-dahs off the walls. Try to keep the noise to a minimum after two in the morning. And no group baths."

"Lavinia, my dear, you're so priggish," says Roddy.

Lavinia rambles on, unperturbed. "Clean sheets and towels once a week, meals included, $250 a month, cash please, and we'll probably ask you to do a few things around the kitchen and the garden."

We have reached the third floor. We stand in a narrow hallway with two doors on the right and two on the left. It is a warm day, but even this close to the roof the house is cool. Through a small, round window at the far end of the hall, I can see the branches of the willow tree shifting in the afternoon air, dappling the walls with green shadows.

"Bathroom is the last door on the right," says Roddy. "This is Tony's room." He raps his knuckles on the first door to our left, grins at Fairfax and me, winks broadly at Tony.

Lavinia clucks, rolls her eyes, and says, "Men."

She points out the remaining two rooms, one on either side of the hall. "These are yours, my dears, though you'll have to decide for yourselves who gets which."

She holds up identical keys, the old-fashioned kind with a hollow handle and a wide, intricate prong at the bottom. "House keys," she says, and hands one to each of us. Then she presses her index finger to her cheek. "Let me see. What have I forgotten?"

Tony smiles. There are prominent dimples in his pale cheeks. "The list of hours, maybe?" he says.

"Ah yes. Breakfast at seven, supper at eight. You're on your own for lunch. But there's tea in Roddy's study every day at five. You're invited, of course."

Then she plucks at Roddy's shirt sleeve. "Come along now. I need you in the kitchen to open some jars for me."

"Lovely, lovely," he says, waving as she tugs him toward the stairs. "So nice to have you here." His voice bounces off the hardwood as he disappears. The sound of it fills me with the same kind of pleasant warmth I used to feel at the orphanage when Sister Mary Rose rocked me after bad dreams.

Tony and Fairfax and I stand grinning at each other in the dusky hallway. Maybe everything will be all right.

I choose the room next to the bathroom, which is just as high and bright as I imagined. The walls are pale green, and the ceiling is slanted. The window is made of small, square panes of beveled glass and has a wide wooden seat beneath it. If the room has any disadvantage at all, it is a view of the sea. In past years, I would have liked nothing better. But since the dreams began, the ocean makes me uneasy at times. I would rather take the other room, the one next to Tony's, which faces the street. But I'm afraid that if the nightmare comes again, I'll disturb Tony, and I would rather he never found out about it.

At first, I live on edge, waiting for the first bad night, anticipating it every time I turn out the lights. But days flow past, and the dream does not return. I begin to relax in spite of myself. We help Roddy patch the roof. I laugh and hammer shingles. I stand square-shouldered and look down on Las Piedras, feeling like the queen of the mountain.

As August turns to September, we help Lavinia pick pomegranates. We crush half the berries in sterilized stone crocks, and Lavinia adds yeast and sugar to start them fermenting into wine. "The finest ritual of the year," she says. We stand in a row at the sink, all of us spattered with crimson juice, tapping feet, knives, and wooden spoons to the beat of rock music from Lavinia's portable tape deck. Tony grins wickedly as he reaches over to dab my nose with his dripping red finger. The kitchen is filled with delicious steam and the smell of boiling stoneware.

The fall semester begins at school. I embark on predicate calculus and non-Euclidean geometry, once again eager and excited by the elegance of mathematics. Time softens the edges of my recollections. Perhaps the nightmare has gone forever; perhaps it wasn't really so bad after all. Only once in all this time does a faint echo of the old terror rise up. One afternoon as I walk home from classes, I notice street names impressed in the concrete curb at the corner just before the house. I'm surprised to discover that the name on the Melville curb does not say Melville. It says *Loma de Viento*. I don't speak Spanish. I don't know what the words mean. Yet as I stand looking down at them, a tingle runs over my scalp. I shake myself and walk home quickly, feeling foolish.

On a chilly evening in mid-October, Tony and Fairfax and I don sweaters and drag wicker chairs from the porch to the front lawn. Warming our fingers around mugs of hot chocolate, we watch an eclipse of the moon. Through shoals of broken clouds, the moon shifts slowly from silver egg to red fingernail, and Tony talks. In a low, drowsy voice, he tells about his work at the physics lab, where they are experimenting with niobium balls, trying to prove the existence of free quarks. We argue, smiling, about whether physics is a field of mathematics, or mathematics is a field of physics. Fairfax asserts that music is the essence of them both.

I keep waiting for him to move closer to her, put his arm around her, idly play with her hair the way men do in paperback romances. But it never happens. In fact, he seems so intent on our discussion of physics and mathematics that he hardly notices anything else. Matters of the heart seem mysterious to me. I am nearly twenty-one years old and still a virgin. Sometimes I wonder if I should have stayed at Our

Lady of the Harbor and joined the Little Sisters of Saint Camillus. Joining a religious order has never been very far from my thoughts. Often, I perceive it as the only right and natural course. It is always Fairfax who convinces me that I should wait a little longer before deciding.

Later, alone in my room, I fall asleep thinking of Tony, his face animated in the glow of the stars and the red moon, the smell of cocoa on his breath, like a little boy. And as hour moves into hour, the nightmare comes again.

This time, the order of the dream events is subtly different from before. I huddle in the black chapel on the deck of the pitching ship. But now one wall of the chapel is a chain-link fence like the one on the orphanage playground. Beyond it stands a man, familiar somehow, clinging to the fence. I can't see his face, but I think it is Tony, bearded, hunched in a sailor's peacoat.

"Electra!" he cries. And he chants the words. "My days are swifter than a weaver's shuttle, and are spent without hope. O remember that my life is wind." Suddenly, I remember such a man from my childhood. It's not Tony. Not Tony at all.

Coming from his lips and not mine, the words have no effect. The wind laughs at him, howls at him. *A bargain is a bargain.* And something else, something new. *Almost of age. Almost mine now.* And it grabs me and spins me around till I scream.

I fancy I can hear the echo of that scream as I awaken. My window stands open, drifting slowly back and forth on its hinges. Under my nightgown, rivulets of sweat run down my ribs. That man. All these years he has lain buried in the clutter of other events, other people. How could I have forgotten about him?

Someone flings open the door. "Electra!" Tony stumbles into the pale rectangle of the doorway. "Jesus . . ." The word comes out of him in a long whisper. "Jesus!"

The horror in his voice makes me look around. Nothing is where it used to be. Pictures have been blown off the walls. Books and papers are strewn everywhere. My bed is upended and lies, frame and mattresses separate, on the floor behind me. My bedclothes stretch in a twisted rope from one corner of the room to the other. Feathers from my pillow fall through the air in lazy eddies.

"What's going on?" Fairfax appears behind Tony, hastily tying the belt of her robe.

I hear urgent footsteps on the stairway and Roddy's voice. "Put that thing away, Lavinia! You'll kill us all." Someone flips the light on. Lavinia lurches into the room, breathless, waving a dusty pistol, and Roddy grabs it from her. Then everyone stands in shocked silence, staring at the wreck of my room.

Fairfax is the first to move. She runs to the window, sticks her head out, looks up and down the backyard. "I don't see anybody," she says. "We must have scared him away." She turns and helps me to my feet.

My head is still spinning from the dream. "It was nobody," I say. "Just the wind. The wind did it." I watch the color leach out of Fairfax's cheeks, and I start to shake. My teeth chatter. It is cold in the room. Without speaking,

Fairfax untwists my blanket and drapes it around my shoulders. I feel her trembling; her hands are moist and chilly.

Tony, dressed in pajamas with tiny, faded fleur-de-lis all over them, scrubs his knuckles across his hair. "The wind? How could the wind do this? It's not even blowing."

Fairfax snaps at him. "Can't you see she's half asleep and scared out of her wits? Of course it wasn't the wind. It was something else."

But Lavinia picks her way across the room and shuts the window. With great authority she says, "Well, it's possible. We do get freak winds up here on the hill sometimes. They used to call this street Loma de Viento, you know, before they decided everything in the neighborhood should have a literary name. So silly."

My scalp prickles again, just as it did when I saw the words in the curb. "Loma de Viento. What does that mean?" I ask in a voice thin and quavery.

Roddy snorts. "It was a bad day indeed when they discontinued the Latin requirement." He emphasizes his words with the barrel of the pistol.

"For heaven's sake, watch where you point that thing," says Lavinia. She turns to me. "Loosely translated, it means Windy Hill, my dear."

In a daze, I watch them put my bed back together. Everyone agrees the question of how it happened is better left for the morning. When Tony and the Desmonds have gone back to their own rooms, Fairfax takes me by the shoulders. "It was the dream, wasn't it?"

I nod.

"Have you ever thought . . . you know, there are people who can move things with their minds. I don't even know what they call it. Psycho-something." She leans toward me. There are fine lines of tension in her forehead. "Electra, I'm afraid for you. You've got to do something about this. Talk to somebody. *Please.*"

I struggle to keep my balance on the wire between laughter and tears. "Who can I talk to? Just tell me. Who knows how to stop the wind?"

"I'm trying to tell you it's not the wind! It's something inside you."

"And I'm trying to tell you it is the wind. Crazy as it sounds, *it is the wind.*"

She lets go of my shoulders and heaves a sigh, one I have heard often before, the one that says, *all right for now, but this isn't settled yet.* "The least you can do is let me stay with you," she says. "I don't think you should be alone tonight."

So we climb into bed together, as we often did when we were little girls. With my head next to hers, I float on the surface of exhausted sleep, thinking about our address. Loma de Viento. 713 Windy Hill. The rational part of me assures the irrational part that it's just a coincidence, that predetermination is an outmoded notion, that nothing from my dark, unknown past has manipulated me into moving to a part of town where there are "freak winds."

These thoughts lead to others, about the man in my dream. I know where the words of the nightmare response came from now. I can almost relive the incident, moment by moment. It is a foggy day on the orphanage playground. I am six years old. I see a man on the other side of the chain-link fence. He is hunched into a big, dark coat. He has a lovely, wild beard and a fisherman's cap with a bill on it. I wander toward him, fascinated. He looks so flat and unreal in the fog. He calls my name. His breath is strong and sour. His voice is strange—husky and broken and wet. He is crying. He whispers the words. "My days are swifter than a weaver's shuttle, and are spent without hope. O remember that my life is wind!" Then he half runs, half stumbles, away into the mist.

Now the dream has brought to mind other forgotten incidents, other times when I have noticed a strange man in a dark coat and a fisherman's cap. Six, seven, a dozen times perhaps. Interspersed throughout my life. The same old seaman watching me, almost always from a distance.

When I wake up the next morning, Fairfax has already slipped away. I hear her practicing the cello in her room down the hall, making a lot of mistakes. She replays the same passages again and again, loudly and impatiently. The day is clear and still, and the sun pours through my window while I pick up rumpled papers, rehang pictures, and replace my battered belongings in their usual cluttered order. There is no permanent damage. Everything looks just as it did before—perhaps a little less dusty.

At breakfast, I dutifully chew and swallow, chew and swallow, and assure everyone that everything is all right. Roddy embarks on a detailed story about the big storm of '58, which uprooted trees, snapped power lines, and left half the houses on Loma de Viento without roofs. Not number

713, he assures us, smiling and stabbing at the yolk of his fried egg. There's not another house in Las Piedras as well built as number 713.

That afternoon, we gather for tea in Roddy's study, my favorite of all the rooms. Its walls look as if they are made of books. A single leaded-glass window and a stone fireplace peek out from among the gold titles and leather bindings. A threadbare Oriental carpet, mostly red, covers the floor. We mill about among the overstuffed chairs, sipping Earl Grey and Lapsang Souchong. Roddy munches gingersnaps and lectures Fairfax on the origins of her name. Nobody says anything about the wind.

"Such a happy quirk of fate," he says. "The name Fairfax comes from the Old English *fyrfeax*, meaning 'fire-haired.'"

A little smile drifts across her face, for the first time today. Fate, of course, had nothing to do with her name, not in the usual way, at least. At Our Lady of the Harbor, Sister Jude, the mother superior, had the duty of naming foundlings. When she was not at prayers or locked away in her office, she spent her time poring over copies of *Beowulf* or the tales of Alfred the king. At vespers, we used to whisper jokes about her. "Sister Jude speaks Old English like a native. Pass it on." "Grendel is Sister Jude's boyfriend. Pass it on."

Roddy turns to me with animation. "You've an interesting name, too," he says.

"What—Thorpe?" I don't know anything about my surname except that Sister Jude chose it, probably on one of her less energetic days. I have always imagined her closing her eyes and pointing, by accident, to the name Thorpe in an open phone book.

"Well . . . Thorpe's interesting, but only vaguely. Comes from *thearf,* meaning 'need' or 'distress.'"

How appropriate for an infant found in the dark on an orphanage stair, with nothing between her skin and the fog but a sailor's tattered peacoat. Maybe I have sold Sister Jude short all these years.

"No, I was thinking more along the lines of Electra," says Roddy. "Now there's a truly fascinating name, don't you agree? I would guess it figures somehow in your family history."

I take a long swallow of hot tea. It seems to go down my throat in an irregular lump. The Desmonds don't know yet about my background or Fairfax's. I wish I could tell Roddy that I am named after my maternal grandmother or a special friend of the family. But the truth is I am only called Electra because that is the name the nuns found scribbled on a bit of soiled canvas in the pocket of my coat-blanket.

"There's not much of a history in my family," I reply, hoping Roddy will become discouraged and move on to some other subject.

But his eyes are bright, and he will not swerve. "Outside the obvious places, the myths and Freud's books and such, I've only come across the name once before. Quite a story. There was an old ship, the *Electra,* used to sail up and down the coast around San Francisco. She was an antique—a barkentine, built to carry cargo, I suppose, but they'd redone her for passengers. Sort of a tourist attraction. She was a lovely sight heading through the Golden Gate. Quite pretty. Doesn't matter if she was old. A lot of old things are pretty." He winks at Lavinia.

Suddenly, the tea is swirling around inside me. It's too hot in the study. I glance toward the window. Maybe I can open it.

Roddy puffs at his pipe. Clouds of sweet-smelling smoke billow in the sunlight. "Quite an amazing story. She got caught in a terrible storm out near the Farallons and actually went to the bottom. November it was. Must be twenty years ago. Let's see. I believe it was the year Sartre declined the Nobel." He studies the ceiling as he works a mental sum. "So it's actually twenty-one years ago now."

He shakes his head. "They should never have had a ship like that out so late in the season. That's what everybody said. Could have been a real disaster, but against all odds, against *incredible* odds, I might even say, the captain got the passengers and crew into lifeboats and saved them all. All but one, that is. A newborn baby, who was lost in the panic somehow. Quite a heroic story. You can imagine what a field day the newspapers had."

A ship with my name, sunk the month I was born, the only fatality a newborn baby. Just a string of coincidences. That's all. A string of coincidences. I repeat the words, but they are empty.

I don't feel very well. My cup slips from my hand. I hear it break as it hits the edge of the table, a distant sound, like the tinkle of wind chimes.

I wobble across the room and unlatch the window. Before I can even push it open, a brutal gust of wind tears it from my hands and flings it outward. The window smashes against the rock wall of the house. Terror roars down my spine in an icy wave.

The carpet has turned into a roiling ocean. I see the ship, masts splintered, sails hanging in rags, wind driving the rain in horizontal sheets. Rain. The air seems full of it. From this wall of black water, Sister Jude emerges, holding out something rectangular and white. But the wind steals my breath, whirls me around like a leaf, and whatever it is she offers me, I can't seem to reach it.

"The window's broken!" Fairfax cries.

Dimly I sense that someone has a strong grip on my arm. I think it is Tony. Or is it the wind? Or is it both of them?

Then the world degenerates into noise. The wind howls. *A bargain is a bargain! Part and parcel!* Beneath that, there is an undercurrent of thuds and crashes, paper tearing and fluttering, the further shattering of glass, and Fairfax screaming my name over and over again.

Then the dream closes in around me, and nothing else seems real.

It's a very long time before I can get the order of the words right. "My days shuttle past, windy life without hope, O remember I am a weaver . . ." Thousands of possibilities, none of them right, till finally one concatenation slips into the darkness like a key into a lock, and I wake up, gasping.

I am lying on my bed, a heavy wool blanket thrown over me. Fairfax dozes on the window seat, her head nodding forward. Tony sits beside me, reading a thick green book, *Paranormal Psychological Phenomena.* It has library reference numbers printed on the spine. There's a purplish bruise beneath one of his eyes and a Band-Aid stuck in his hair.

"What happened to you?" I say.

He looks up, startled at first; then his dimples appear and his cheeks turn red. "Oh nothing," he says. "Hey, Fairfax. She's awake."

Fairfax snaps upright, her eyes full of sleepy confusion. Through the window behind her, I can see that it's dark outside. I hear the distant braying of the foghorn on Las Piedras Point. The house has a peculiar, muffled feeling about it, as if it's wrapped in cotton.

"How long have I been asleep?" I ask.

"Hours," says Fairfax. "Do you remember what happened?"

"No. It was noisy. I opened the window. I've been dreaming, haven't I?"

"It was more than a dream," says Tony. "The library's a shambles. Roddy and Lavinia are still downstairs putting books away and sweeping up glass."

I imagine Lavinia's china teacups pounded to shards, the beautiful leather books lying bent and torn on the Oriental carpet, and kindly, whimsical old Roddy picking each one up and dusting it off like an injured child. What have they done to deserve this?

I sit up and test my feet against the floor. I feel as if I've been beaten with a board. "I'm going to the orphanage," I say. "I've got to talk to Sister Jude." But when I try to stand up, my knees buckle and I fall back onto the bed.

"Take it easy," says Tony. "Here. You've been tossing and turning so much your pillow's like a rock. Let me fluff it up for you." He bats at the pillow clumsily, his worried gaze never leaving my face. "Fairfax told me all about this orphanage of yours. One thing's for sure. It's too far to go in the fog."

Fairfax rises abruptly, hands clenched, thumbs inside her fists. "Electra, there's a professor in the psychology department who's interested in problems like yours. I think we should go see him. The orphanage can wait till tomorrow."

I take a long breath. I remember how we used to argue about the difference between that which is incomprehensible and that which is impossible. I could never make her believe in the square roots of negative numbers, or in infinities, or even in the empty set. "Even nothing is something," she would say. Perhaps the notion of wind as a conscious entity is just as difficult.

"I don't need a psychologist, Fairfax. I need to see Sister Jude."

"How the hell do you know?" She is trembling, and the veins in her neck stand out. "Do you realize that Tony almost got killed this afternoon shielding you from flying glass and books? And here you are, blabbering about going to see some half-witted nun who's so far away from the real world that she probably doesn't even care what year it is. You know, there are other people's lives in danger here! It's not just you anymore." She almost screams the last sentence.

By the time she finishes, I am trembling, too, and working my fists around inside my pockets to keep from lashing out at her.

Tony touches my arm. "Look, Electra. I don't know anything about parapsychology." He gestures toward the thick green book with the library numbers. "I'm not sure I even believe in it. But I am a scholar. And I do know that when you've got a specific problem, the best way to start on a solution is to track down every lead you can find—even the wildest. Maybe Fairfax is right. Maybe this guy can help you figure out what's going on. How will you ever know if you don't go see him?"

Track down every lead, even the wildest. I almost smile at the irony of Tony's words. I look out the window at the gray wall of fog. Somewhere beyond it, beating the waves into foam, whistling among the offshore rocks, the wind is waiting for me. The marrow of my bones is cold with eerie certainty that the wind means to kill anyone who tries to keep it from getting what it wants. There is no time left for pride.

I sit up very straight. "Take me to the orphanage. Just take me up there, and I promise I'll go see the psychologist tomorrow."

Fairfax sticks her jaw out. "What can anybody at Our Lady of the Harbor possibly do that a psychologist can't do better?"

"They can tell me about my past."

Fairfax swallows, and is silent.

Roddy and Lavinia watch from the porch as we slide into the front seat of Tony's car. "Won't you reconsider? It's a terrible night for driving," says Lavinia.

Roddy rubs her gently on the back and waves to us. "Be very careful," he says.

Tony calls out across the misty yard, "Don't worry. We'll be home before you know it." Then he turns the key in the ignition.

"Sorry," he says, as the engine rumbles to life. "The top has been stuck in the down position ever since I bought it. I haven't had time to fix it yet." He flicks the heater switch to high.

It's not far to San Francisco. On a clear day, it takes only thirty or forty minutes to get there. But tonight is different. The fog is so thick it even diffuses the dashboard lights. For all I can tell, we are sitting in a parked car with a fan blowing on our faces. Tony assures me we are moving at a steady twenty miles per hour. I don't know whether to curse the fog for slowing us down or to pray that it won't disappear. It is an omen. A signal. As long as it surrounds us, I know the wind is far away.

It is almost ten-thirty when we reach Our Lady of the Harbor. Adobe walls loom out of the night, full of dark windows. The hour of the compline is long past, but the Little Sisters of Saint Camillus never turn away visitors in need.

There is always someone on duty. Tony, Fairfax, and I huddle before the massive door and ring the night bell.

We wait a moment, listening for footsteps, hearing only the creak of moorings on the nearby wharf. I wonder how many nights, as a child, I lay in my bed and listened to this very sound.

It seems hours before a voice comes from behind the tiny, barred door-window. "Who rings our bell?"

"Electra Thorpe, Mary Fairfax, and a friend," I say.

"Electra? Mary Fairfax?" Bolts are shot back, the door thrown open, and there stands Sister Michael. A smile creeps across her pale, abstracted face. We have probably pulled her from some private prayer. She hugs us and draws us through the vestibule toward the library. "You look so cold, poor dears. But how wonderful to see you! Come, come. I have a fire lit. I was just reading Saint Augustine. Are you familiar with him?"

Tony laughs softly. "Philosophy 101. He tried to prove that good is more powerful than evil."

"Yes. And he succeeded. At least as far as the Church was concerned," says Sister Michael. She smiles at him with increased warmth and a curious tilt of her head.

Fairfax flounces into a patched and worn chair near the fire. She's so cold her lips are blue, and it takes her a moment to work her face into a sarcastic grin. "See, Electra? You have nothing to worry about. Good will eventually triumph."

"What do you mean, my child?" says Sister Michael.

Fairfax crosses her arms and slouches deeper into the chair. "Ask them."

Sister Michael raises inquiring eyes toward me, face half shadowed by her brown wimple.

I meet the gaze steadily, as I have done few times in my life. "I'm sorry, Sister. There's no time to explain. I've come to see Sister Jude. It's urgent."

She looks at me quizzically. "What an odd coincidence. She's been trying to find you."

I attempt to swallow the dryness in my throat. "I didn't realize."

She nods. "Sister Jude is ill. She had a mild stroke last month, you know. Unless it's extremely important, I'd rather not wake her. I could take your address and phone number . . ."

Panic spurts through me. "A stroke? Will she be all right? It's not serious, is it?"

"There's no real need to worry. She was only in the hospital for a few days, but it has slowed her down. You know how these things go."

"I understand, but . . . please, I . . . please. It *is* important."

She contemplates me for a moment, touching the tips of her fingers together, moving them apart, touching them together again. I wonder what she sees in my face. I wonder if the fear moves under the skin of my cheeks in visible waves. She nods once more. But this time she rises and walks toward the door. "Wait here," she says.

She is gone a long time. We sit in silence, listening to the clock on the mantel. It's an expensive one—an antique, probably a gift from some successful parishioner. Its intricate workings click away in plain view beneath a glass bell. I remember the stream of gifts that used to come through the orphanage door every Christmas. Half a dozen lovely trees. Cases of wine and olive oil and wheels of cheese. Boxes of nuts and dried fruit, crates of brilliant oranges.

The clock strikes eleven, and we hear the shuffle of slippers on the stone floor. "Here we are," says Sister Michael as she guides Sister Jude into the room.

Sister Jude has always been old, but now she looks truly ancient. Her spine is bent. She watches her feet with great concentration as she hobbles along, leaning on a knobby black cane. She is wearing a frayed brown bathrobe. Silver hair peeks out from under her wimple.

When she is settled in one of the chairs by the fire, she tilts her head up with an effort. A smile whispers across her face. "Greetings, Electra. Have you come to join us after all?"

I look down at the floor. My cheeks burn.

"How did you know I've been thinking of you?" Her left eyelid droops, dead and unmoving, but her right eye shines in the glow of the fire.

"I had a dream," I say. "In the dream, you wanted to give me something."

Sister Michael makes a small sound—almost a whimper—and presses her fist to her mouth. She sways slightly, and Tony reaches out to steady her.

"What's wrong?" I ask. "Are you all right?"

The good half of Sister Jude's face tightens into a look of vague and lopsided pain. "Perhaps we have witnessed a miracle," she says. "I tried to contact you, but the university has no record of your current address. I prayed that God would send you here." A soft, dry laugh whispers from her throat. "I have spent my life believing that the age of miracles was past."

She reaches into the pocket of her robe and pulls out a white envelope, torn open along the top. She hands it to me. "Forgive me for opening it. It was marked urgent, and when I couldn't reach you . . ."

I turn it over and over, struggling against a rush of déjà vu. I read the front. *Electra, c/o Little Sisters of Saint Camillus, Home for Children, San Francisco, California.* It's the kind of envelope you can buy in any drugstore, ten for a dollar. The return address says *Jimmy's Tavern, Mission Street, San Francisco.* The word *urgent* runs in capital letters along the bottom edge. The writing is shaky but clear.

Inside the envelope is a sheet of binder paper, buckled as if it has gotten wet somehow.

"Dear Electra," it says. "Time is getting short by now. Nearly your twenty-first birthday, and that was the bargain. I've got no right to ask you favors. But it chews at my soul, what I did, and I can't go to my grave without telling you. If God has any mercy, you'll find me at Jimmy's in the Mission. Any night this week. Ask for Captain Fletcher."

The paper flutters out of my hand.

"What does it say?" Fairfax springs from her chair and snatches the letter from the floor. Tony reads over her shoulder.

"What's the postmark?" he says. "When was it mailed?"

I am still holding the envelope, forgotten, between the fingers of my left hand. Tony takes it from me, glances at the stamp, then at his watch. "This is dated Monday, October thirteenth. Today's the fifteenth—almost the sixteenth. He'll still be there." He looks up at me. There are lines in his face I have never seen before. "Who is this guy, anyway?"

I try to make some answer, but I can't think of any. My chin is quivering, and the only communication I can manage is a shrug.

"I'll bet he's her father, the son of a bitch!" says Fairfax. "How could he be so cruel?"

"Why is it cruel, Mary?" says Sister Jude. "If he is her father, it is not cruelty that makes him write this letter. It is only human nature, and one of the better parts at that."

I kneel down beside Sister Jude's chair. "Please," I say. "What do you know about me? About him? Tell me about that night, the night they found me here."

She smiles. I remember that smile, surprisingly small for all the love it contains. She strokes my hair. Her hand is rough and bony. "I'm sorry, Electra. There is little to tell about you—about any of our children."

"There must be something. *Something.*"

She lifts her chin just slightly, and the creases in her forehead deepen. In my mind an image of her appears, a small brown figure gazing up at mountains of dust, each speck of dust a memory. I have never felt as minuscule as I do at this moment.

"I remember the way we named you," she says. "You were wrapped in a seaman's coat, and in it we found a scrap of sailcloth. 'Electra,' it said. We believe you were named after a ship. A ship that sank. Did you know that?"

I shake my head. I wonder how fast the hearts of mice beat, or hummingbirds. No faster than mine.

"Well. It seemed so fitting. The *Electra* sank just before you came, and a child aboard her was killed. We thought of you as a living memorial to that child's soul."

I rest my throbbing forehead against the arm of the chair. The wood feels cool and good.

"You arrived in November. During the storm in which the ship was lost."

"My birthday is November seventeenth. It must have been after that."

"No . . . no, we celebrate a foundling's birthday on the anniversary of his arrival. So although you came to us in the middle of November, your real birthday must have been well before that. As much as a month, I'm sure." She smiles distantly. "I have never seen a baby before or since whose eyes were so bright. The world fascinated you."

I barely hear the last part. I'm busy developing several meticulous proofs. They all conclude the same way. If Sister Jude is right, I'm a month older than I thought. My twenty-first birthday might be today, or yesterday, or tomorrow, instead of next month.

"Sister Jude, do you have any idea who wrote this letter?" says Tony.

She shakes her head. "None. As Fairfax says, her father, perhaps."

Slowly a thought has been percolating its way through my subconscious. Now it flows into place among all the other thoughts. "He's the man in the fog," I say. "The sailor outside the playground fence. I'm certain of it. I've got to find him. The sooner the better."

"*What* man in the fog?" says Fairfax.

"A man I saw when I was a little girl. I dreamed about him the night of the eclipse. And now I remember seeing him more than once. Watching. Just watching."

Tony turns toward me, his face oddly soft in the firelight. "Electra, you know there are some pretty crazy people hanging around the Mission district. Why don't you let me find him for you, talk to him, make sure he's not planning to . . . to hurt you somehow."

I lay my hand on his shoulder, touching him for the first time, thinking about it only after I have done it. Even through his shirt and his tattered sweater, he feels warm. Maybe it's just that my hands are so cold. "Thank you. But I don't think there's time." I almost whisper it.

Fairfax takes two steps toward me, stops, clenches her fists. "Don't go, Electra. I'm afraid. This feels all wrong."

I smile at her. I can feel it on the inside of my face, like the heat of a tiny flame against a wall. "You know how it is, Fairfax. I know you do. He can tell me who I am."

She never cries. Not even now. But her eyes are very bright as she nods slowly.

I take Sister Jude's hands between my own. I have known her all my life and now I am leaving. What can I say that will not be inadequate?

But she speaks before I can. "I think you'll be back," she says.

My throat is so tight I can barely answer. "I will if I can. I promise."

She gazes at me with her one piercing eye. "Take my crucifix," she says, leaning forward so I can unfasten the chain around her neck. Her voice is full of hard, icy authority, the kind no one denies.

"Yes, Sister," I say automatically, as I have countless times before, when the lessons and commands were not as important as now. I reach out and release the catch. The crucifix is small, made of dark wood, hand-carved with intricate designs. I fasten the chain around my own neck.

"There is a line in the poem of the Wanderer," she says. " '*Til bith he-the his treowe ye-healdeth.*' It means, 'Good is he who keeps his pledges.'"

I nod, scrubbing my eyes on the sleeve of my coat, and Tony and Fairfax and I walk away toward the heavy door and the fog beyond it. The clock strikes twelve.

"I will if I can," I murmur.

I count the street lamps as we start down Mission Street. Three, five, seven. In the fog, which seems thinner now, they begin as nebulous clouds of light and grow to bright spheres with halos. I see fewer and fewer of them as we get further east, closer to the piers where the big ships tie up. Twenty-one. I turn the number over in my mind, wondering what makes it so special. Not a prime. Not a square. Three sevens. Three for the trinity, seven because it is magic and has been magic since time began.

Jimmy's is a single-story dive on a deserted corner. Above the grimy front window, a neon sign blinks on and off, first a naked pink woman, then a green palm tree. We don't even have to look for a parking spot.

Tony presses his palm lightly against the cracked plastic doorplate, then looks at me worriedly.

Fairfax clutches my sleeve and says, "Are you sure about this?"

The faintest whisper of a breeze tickles my cheeks. The fog is lifting. "Hurry," I say.

Tony pushes through the doorway into the darkness of the tavern. At first I can't see anything. The smell of stale beer and rum is so powerful that it makes my stomach squirm. There's a jukebox playing softly, something nondescript, a female vocalist singing about how she can't get along without love. I hear Tony trip over something—probably a wooden stool—as he makes his way up to the bar.

There are candles in round red glasses on each table. By their meager light, I can just make out the bartender, a huge man, wiping a mug on his apron. "Whadya want?" he says.

"We're looking for someone named Captain Fletcher," says Tony. "He said we could find him here."

The bartender snorts and inclines his head toward the back of the room.

We make our way among the rickety tables where scattered patrons drink alone or in pairs. In an isolated corner, far from the door, a wild-haired figure sits hunched over a shot glass and a pint bottle of whiskey.

"Captain Fletcher?" says Tony.

"Who the hell are you?" says the man, wrapping his arms around his bottle as if to protect it.

"I've brought Electra."

There's a sound of indrawn breath, then a sigh, almost a sob. "Figured she'd be gone by now," he says.

I push a chair out of the way and sit down opposite him. I stare at his face, trying to match it with the face outside the playground fence. There are too many wrinkles and not enough light. All I get is an eerie sense of the familiar, without being able to pinpoint it.

I take a deep breath. There's a simple test that will settle the matter. "My days are swifter than a weaver's shuttle," I say, "and are spent without hope."

In the glow of the red candle, tears spill over his cheeks, and he hides his face with his arms. He moans softly. "O remember that my life is wind: mine eye shall no more see good."

"What does it mean?" I whisper. "I've been dreaming it for months."

He gazes at me miserably. "Sweet Christ. In the last twenty-one years I've nearly memorized the whole damn Book of Job. That's where it's from, if you want to know. They might as well have written it for me. God only knows how many times I've asked Him to either kill me or forgive me and be done with it."

"Forgive you for what?" says Fairfax, leaning toward him, teeth bared as if she would like to grab him by the collar and shake him till his neck breaks. "You've done something to Electra, haven't you! Is that what needs forgiving?"

Tony pulls her away. She jerks herself from his grip and stands trembling beside me, glaring at the old seaman.

Captain Fletcher throws back his head and laughs. "I've done something to Electra? That's a good one. *Which* Electra? There are far too many in this piss hole of a world."

Suddenly I notice a small sound, barely audible except to one who is listening for it—a breeze gently scrabbling at the window of Jimmy's Tavern. My mouth goes dry.

"Are you my father?"

He's still laughing, almost helplessly, at some joke nobody else can see. "Your father?" he says. "If I were your father, this would all have been much simpler, wouldn't it now?"

I realize I've been holding my breath. I let it out now, embarrassed at the relief I feel. My father is a better man than Fletcher. I can still dream of that.

"You said if God had any mercy, I'd find you. Well, I have," I say. "And I want to know what you meant about bargains, and time getting short."

His laughter stops as abruptly as it started, and his eyes cloud up. He's full of booze, I tell myself. A soppy, pitiful drunk. I try not to despise him for his weakness. Whatever he's done, he hates himself for it. That should be enough.

"Twenty-one years ago, I was the captain of a ship," he says. "A ship named *Electra*. A fine, stinking ship that went to the bottom in a storm. Nobody died. Not a soul! You want to know why? Because I made a bargain with the wind."

I sit at the table, frozen, as the story of my beginnings comes out at last.

"I took you from your mother's arms. In the confusion, your parents never knew what happened. I told them you were washed overboard, but I hid you in the bow of a lifeboat, underneath a sail bag. And I used you to buy our lives. Used you for a bargaining chip. Every sailor knows. The wind is always interested if there's a soul involved. Especially a child's soul. Something new and pretty it can gloat over."

For a long moment, while it all soaks in, nobody speaks. Then Fairfax leans across the table and says in a voice too thin to be convincing, "That's a lot of bull."

Tony, his face tight, scrutinizes Captain Fletcher. "I don't believe you. If you're telling the truth, why didn't the wind take her then, on the spot? Why wait until now?"

The captain flashes him a crazy grin. "Wind can't take a person's soul against his will. Or so the story goes. It's a matter that can't be decided till the age of majority."

"You mean all Electra has to do is say, *No, you can't have me?*" says Tony, his voice breaking with anger and incredulity.

The captain shrugs and starts to lift his bottle. Tony reaches out and stops him.

"You're making all this up, right? I mean, what kind of bargain is that?"

The captain answers softly. "What do you take me for? Listen for yourself. Does that sound like an old man's imagination?"

Tony turns his head, just slightly. He hears it, too—the wind again, more insistent this time, whistling at the keyhole, curling around the garish sign outside, making it tap against the bricks.

"It made me promise she'd be brought up right—kept clean and perfect till the time. That's why I gave her to the nuns," says Fletcher, his dazed eyes focused on something far away, something none of us can see. "The wind has its ways of stacking the deck. Just like anybody else. It's been sniffing around her all along, whispering about how she should like some things and hate others, trying to persuade her she's got nothing to lose. But that's not the worst of it."

He lifts his bottle with trembling hands and takes a long pull. This time, Tony makes no move to stop him. "What do you think will happen to me if she says no? What do you think will happen to you and everybody else she gives a damn about? Ask her. I'm sure she knows by now." He shakes his head. "You can't imagine the kinds of death the wind can think up for a man, even if you've seen them with your own eyes."

Fairfax is on her feet, flailing at the air while Tony holds her back. "You son of a bitch! What gave you the right to gamble away somebody else's soul? *Your* soul. It should have been *your* soul!"

"*My* soul? You stinking brat. You don't know much about bargains, do you? Why should the wind take mutton when it can have lamb instead?" This time when he laughs it fills the whole room, a horrible, deranged hooting sound, almost a cry of pain. When it's over, he wipes spittle on his sleeve and takes another long drink. "And as for what gave me the right, it was numbers. Simple, stinking numbers." He winks at me as if we are members of the same conspiracy. "You know all about numbers, don't you, my girl. Think you love 'em, eh? Think you know all about them. Well look what they've done to *me!*"

I push back my chair, rise from it unsteadily, too numb to feel the floor beneath my feet. "What do you mean?"

"I mean it's all in the numbers. A hundred and twenty-nine to one. A hundred and twenty-nine men, women, and children, sunk to Davy Jones. Or one baby girl . . . one baby girl . . ."

I back away, tipping over the chairs, bumping into tables.

Outside, the wind has risen to a shriek. The walls shake. The windows rattle in their frames.

"It's a lie!" Fairfax screams. "Everything he said is a lie!"

How I wish I could believe her.

The other patrons, mostly sailors and whores, have begun to rise from their tables and grope toward the walls with the edgy jerkiness of impending panic. The bartender glances up at the ceiling, raises an arm to shield his head from bits of falling plaster, then whirls toward me and shouts, "You! Get outa my bar!"

"Stop!" says Tony. "Don't go any closer to the door." And he throws himself over the clutter of tables and chairs to seize me by the wrist.

I am lost in a wasteland of fears and confusions. I want to live. I want to find my mother and father. I want to feel what it's like to be someone with an inherited past, long and complicated and rich. It isn't fair. It isn't fair.

At the same time I think of the way I used to look up at the stars and wonder why I was different—an introvert, cold and frightened at a man's touch, ecstatic only at the laws of mathematics. I held the hope of change inside me like a candle in a lantern. Now I see the truth. I am different because my soul has never been my own. Maybe I will never change. Maybe I cannot.

I stare at Tony's fingers curled tight around my wrist, and I cry, "Don't let go of me! Oh God, yes, let go of me!"

"Electra!" His eyes are rimmed with tears. "People care about you. All of us care—Fairfax, Roddy, Lavinia, *me*. You can't just give up. *I love you, Electra!* I won't let you go."

I have only an instant to feel astonished at his words, only an instant to wonder at the way they rekindle the candle in the lantern. Then the front window splinters into a million pieces. Tony's face is suddenly speckled with blood. He closes his eyes tight and staggers backward with a cry of surprise. As if from a great distance, I hear the other customers shouting, screaming. My clothes are plastered flat against my body. The wind is pulling at me, and the inside of my skull vibrates with the message I have come to know by heart: *A bargain is a bargain, part and parcel.*

Fairfax launches herself at me, wraps her arms around one of my legs as the wind drags me toward the door. "Don't go! He said you don't have to go," she shrieks. The mirror behind the bar bursts outward in a spray of deadly shards.

The pieces of my life hang in the air before me. Bits which have always seemed random before coalesce now into something whole, something with a shape—not elegant or beautiful, but pleasing nonetheless, and powerful somehow. I think of Sister Jude bent over her books, of Fairfax practicing the cello with her eyes closed, of my dusty hats and boxes of pretty buttons, warm days spent on windy beaches, Roddy's suspenders and Lavinia's pomegranate wine, the completeness theorem, Tony DiMarini, who says he loves me, smiling and sipping cocoa by the light of a lunar eclipse. Every person, every place, every event, speeding toward one point in time: this moment of choice.

I look down at Fairfax, clinging to my ankle, her hair like a mane of flames, streaked now with dark blood. Behind her, Tony has fallen to all fours, shaking his head as if to clear it. With a fresh spurt of terror, I understand exactly what the wind wants. It wants me to believe that Captain Fletcher is right. That it's a simple matter of numbers. My life in return for the lives of those I love. But it's not just my life the wind is after. It's my soul. And if I succumb, it will be worse than death. Much worse.

Tony climbs back to his feet and tackles me like a football player, grabbing frantically for a hold the wind can't break. But slowly, slowly, I feel myself slipping away from him. "Don't let go, Tony, oh God, don't let go!" I scream, and I squeeze my eyes shut. The darkness magnifies the sting of plaster and bits of glass peppering my skin. But it's better than seeing.

I am already far beyond surprise when, through the blackness and the incredible din, I hear a whisper. "I think you will be back." I almost feel the brush of lips against my ear. The voice is Sister Jude's. In that moment, the chaos of the external world recedes, and I think, *Of course. Why didn't I see it before?* And I remember that any equation can be solved in a number of ways and that often the most elegant paths to solution are the least obvious.

I open my eyes, and the chaos roars in again. I throw up an arm to protect my face, and the words come to me as if I've always known them. I cry into the wind. "Mary, Mother of God, intercede for me. To Our Holy Father I offer my life in service as His bride!"

The wind stops completely, as if my words have shocked it somehow. But only for the barest instant. Then it rises again with a noise like a freight train, a howl that makes me clap my hands to my head. The air pressure in the bar drops abruptly. *The roof's blowing off,* I find myself thinking

calmly. There's a shower of concrete and an oddly inconse-
quential wash of pain, mental or physical, perhaps both,
muffled and diluted by the gradual loss of consciousness.

In our mountain valley, the sun is rising. I pause, kneeling
at matins, to look out through the window of the chapel.
The peaks above the convent, already touched with copper
brilliance, stand out hard-edged against the deep blue sky.
The upper reaches of the forest shimmer in a golden halo of
light. I like this view, an orderly one, full of God's own for-
mulations. It is far removed from the sea, a good place to
make a new start, especially when one is named after a
ship.

My hand goes to my neck and Sister Jude's crucifix, one
of the few worldly possessions I brought with me when I
came here. I ask for strength. I still can't think of my past
without a stab of yearning, as if I have cut myself on a small,
sharp jewel that will never wear smooth. No one died at
Jimmy's Tavern except Captain Fletcher. He, and only he,
lost his life when the roof blew off, while the rest of us were
spared. All of those I love in that other world remain.

Letters come at intervals. Sister Michael writes that
Sister Jude spends her days dozing in the sun. From Roddy
and Lavinia I receive news of good books and the condition
of the garden. Lavinia never fails to mention the two boxes of
small treasures I asked her to keep for me in the moments
before I left, unable, though I tried with all my might, to
assign them to the trash bin.

Fairfax and Tony write seldom. They are more likely to

appear at our door every few months, bearing gifts of pomegranate wine, warm scarves for the snowy winter, or varieties of fresh fruit we cannot raise ourselves at these elevations. If the day is warm, I walk with them in the woods. If not, we sit together in the public room, where a fire keeps the chill away.

Fairfax talks about her music, which consumes her now as it never did before. On each occasion, she has discovered something new—a special technique, the name of an unknown composer, or the fresh interpretation of a particular phrase.

But Tony never talks about his work. Instead, he always asks, the look in his eyes a little less hopeful each time, "Will you ever leave this place?"

And I always reply, "No, Tony. I won't."

It is then that I feel the most pain from the little, sharp jewel of yearning and I push it away, wrap it in the protection of rationality, and seize the truth. This life is right for me. And even if it were not, a bargain is a bargain, part and parcel.

THE TUCKAHOE

It's getting on towards dark, and I keep hoping maybe I've caught a fever and I'm out of my head. Maybe there isn't anything waiting under the house to get me as soon as I step outside. Maybe Pa and Lemmy are just playing a trick on me, and they'll come strutting through the front door any minute now, smug as a couple of tom turkeys. Oh, how I'd like that. Pa, he'd laugh at me, because that's his way, to make a joke out of Ruben, who'll never be a man. And Lemmy would probably hook his thumbs in his belt and call me his sissy little brother, seeing me wrapped up in Momma's quilt like this, shaking, and nothing sticking out except my nose and the barrel of Grampa's Colt pistol. But I wouldn't mind. It would be all right, just this once. If they came in here alive and whole, if they could prove tuckahoe is just tuckahoe, and that empty thing on the porch isn't really what's left of Momma. Then they could laugh all they want, and it would be all right. Just this once.

The rain started in again a couple hours ago, just like last night. Makes my heart crawl up into my throat and lie there twitching like a half-dead frog. I lit all the lamps and tried to make a fire in the fireplace. But the fire, it won't seem to burn right. It looks just the way I feel, puny and wavery, like it might not be here in the morning. I tried to give myself a good talking-to, just like Momma would if she saw me now. "Ruben," she would say, "the Lord helps them that helps themselves." But I don't think the Lord had much to do with this rain, nor with the thing that ate Momma.

Last night, when the storm first started, I had a feeling this wasn't any regular rain. Didn't seem natural the way it poured out of the sky. It came down in long, wavy curtains, like somebody'd emptied a bunch of big tin washtubs all at one time. There weren't any drops at all except from the splashes when it hit the ground. And the lightning felt wrong, too. I've never seen such lightning before. Why, it lit up the sky blue and white all night long, one bolt right after another. Early on in the evening, I saw it hit the two big old poplars down by the road, both at the same time. Before the rain put the fire out, they were burnt to pure cinders, and there was nothing left this morning except black poles.

The thing that made my skin creep worst of all, though, was the smell. I mostly like the smell of rain, especially this time of year, when the tree sap is running and the ground is already a little damp. But this smelled funny, kind of like that oily stuff Pa sprays on the crops sometimes to kill the bugs. I told Pa that. I said the rain smelled real bad, like oil or something. I even went out on the porch and got a little on my fingers so he could smell it for himself.

But Pa, he has a stubborn streak, and most times he doesn't pay any attention till something turns around and bites him right on the toe. He looked at me kind of sideways, scratching his beard, and he said, "Ruben, I don't smell a blame thing. Quit acting like an old woman." And Lemmy made it worse by laughing outright.

I saw right then I might as well not waste any more breath on those two, so I just shut my mouth and went over to the table to watch Momma kneading bread. I like to watch her when she has her sleeves rolled up and her hands all covered with flour. Sometimes a lock of fine, brown hair falls down in her eyes, and she asks me if I'll tuck it back for her. Last night, when I tucked her hair back in, she whispered, "The rain don't smell right to me, neither, if you want to know the truth." Remembering that now makes me feel like crying.

After a while, I lay down by the fire and tried to read in one of my schoolbooks about this fellow who discovered the South Pole, but it was no use. I kept getting this stickery feeling all up and down my back. Made me think Lemmy or somebody had sneaked up behind me and was trying to scare me. But every time I twisted around to look, there was nobody there at all, just the front window lit up all cold and blue, and the curtains of rain outside, and the roar of thunder. The more I stared at that book, the more I thought about the window, and the queerer I felt about what I might see through it if I turned around again. The hairs on my arms and the back of my neck stood up, and pretty soon a cold sweat broke out on my lip, right where I'm starting to get a few little mustache hairs. I made up my mind the only way to get myself over being afraid was to go take a good long look through the window to prove there was nothing peering in, fearsome or otherwise.

I put my book down on the rug where I'd been lying, and I got up and walked to the window, which was misted over a little on account of its being warmer inside than out. I spit on my sleeve and rubbed a little place in the glass. I couldn't see too good, because the rain and lightning made everything look so different. The straw grass on the front acre might have been a stranger's pond, and Momma's chicken coop loomed up in the night like one of those dinosaurs I've seen in books. I squinted for a long time, and finally after I had things figured out a little, I saw the chickens were all riled up, flapping around in the rain. That struck me as just plain unnatural, for chickens are pretty much like people when it comes to staying indoors on a wet night.

Then I saw the other thing, and it gave me a chill so deep I felt like I'd been dropped down a well. Through that little place in the glass, I made out something creeping towards the root cellar. I stood still as a lump of salt to get a better look, though my blood was hammering inside my veins, and my knees felt like cheese. The next bolt of lightning lit up everything almost as clear as day, and just for a second, even with the rain, I got a perfect sight of the thing.

There's a funny kind of toadstool that grows down in the dimmest part of the woods. Tuckahoe, Pa calls them, but Momma says they aren't like any tuckahoe she ever saw, and we aren't to eat them under any circumstances. I wouldn't want to anyway, for the sight of them puts me off my feed. You never find just one or two, coming up separate around dead wood like regular mushrooms. These tuckahoe like to grow from the heart of a living tree, a hundred or more together in a slippery, gray clump, like overgrown frogs' eggs. No single one of them is bigger than a man's thumb, but I have often seen nests two feet around stuck onto unlucky maples and dogwoods. Lemmy, he gets bored sometimes and knocks the clumps down and hacks them up with a stick for fun. But me, I'd rather stay as far away from them as I can.

Tuckahoe. That's what I thought of as I watched that thing crawl across our front acre in the stinking rain. I felt the sweat gathering into little streams on my forehead while I told myself to stop and think. It couldn't be tuckahoe because it was too big, big as a man. Besides that, it was moving, and fast, too. Tuckahoe couldn't move by itself, not that I ever heard of anyway.

I could feel a howl building up in my throat, getting ready to come out whether I wanted it to or not, when all of a sudden there was a big crash from the back of the house and the whole place shook. I think I did let out a yell then, but nobody paid any attention because they were all running to see what had caused the commotion. By the time I got my wits together enough to follow them, Pa and Lemmy were standing by the back door looking out into the storm. A good-sized limb from the old oak tree by the kitchen had torn loose in the wind and come down on the roof. Pa was growling and cursing, and Momma was out in the rain with a *Farm Journal* over her head, trying to see if the roof was all right.

All I could think of was that thing crawling around out there, and I says, "Get her back inside! Get her out of the rain!" My voice cracked, just like it always does when I most wish it wouldn't.

And Lemmy gave me one of those cockeyed half smiles of his and said, "For Pete's sake. You'd think she's made of sugar or something. The rain ain't gonna melt her, you know."

Then I hit Lemmy in the stomach, and he hit me in the nose. And the next thing I knew, Momma was standing over me with an ice pack, yelling a blue streak, and dripping rainwater all over the kitchen floor. I didn't care. I just closed my eyes and let her yell. As long as she was back inside, that's all that mattered to me.

This morning, I remember lying in bed thinking the tuckahoe thing must have been nothing but a bad dream. I heard birds chirping outside the window and I watched a little finger of sunlight move across a spider web in the corner. The rain had stopped, and the clouds were no more than a few raggedy strings way up high. I felt so good that I whistled while I put my pants on and said good morning to Lemmy even though my nose was still pretty sore.

Momma was getting ready to go out and fetch the eggs from the chickens, like she does every morning. She had to pull on a pair of high rubber boots, because the front acre was ankle-deep in mud from the storm. I stood in the sunshine on the porch and watched her wade out towards the chicken coop. She had a basket hanging from one arm for the eggs. She got about ten or fifteen steps away, then stopped dead still with the basket swinging from her elbow. She turned around, and the look on her face made me swallow without meaning to.

"There's something kind of funny out here, Ruben," she said. "Better ask Pa to come and take a look."

I hollered for Pa, and he grumbled, for he hates to get up from his chair. But he lumbered out into the mud, and me and Lemmy rolled up our pants and followed him.

Momma had come across a patch of slimy stuff. It could have been egg whites maybe, except it was sort of milky, and where would egg whites come from anyway, there being no yolks or shells lying around? Pa frowned at it, and Lemmy and him stuck their fingers in it. Then Pa said it wasn't anything to worry about, probably some new kind of bug left it, or it might be some kind of mildew, he didn't know.

All that time, I was standing on one foot and then the other, and my heart was ticking as fast as a two-dollar watch. I had a pretty fair idea what had left that slime, and it didn't have anything to do with bugs. "Pa," I said, "I think you should know I saw some kind of strange critter crawling around out here last night, looked like one of those tuckahoe clumps, only almost as big as you are."

Lemmy rolled his eyes and spit in the mud right by my foot. Pa just looked mad and said, "Ruben, everybody knows you can't tell the difference between a tall tale and the truth. If you think I'm gonna swallow a story like that, you got a brain about the size of a pea." Then him and Lemmy sloshed back to the house, talking and laughing. I stayed outside with Momma, because I felt like I was either going to throw things or cry, and I didn't want to give Pa the satisfaction of seeing it.

By and by, me and Momma went and took a look at the chicken coop. It turned out there were hardly any eggs in the boxes. That was spooky enough. But what we found just inside the chicken wire scared me a lot worse. I thought I saw two rags lying there on the ground, but when I looked closer, I saw it wasn't rags at all. It was two dead hens, just their feathers and skin, with nothing inside. I squinted and poked, but I couldn't find any rips or bites. It was like all the blood and meat and bones had been sucked right out of them, leaving them empty, without a single mark.

Momma turned all white when she saw those hens, and she told Pa about them as soon we got back inside. But he treats her the same way as he treats me, like she hasn't got the sense she was born with. He said to her, "What do you expect after a storm like that? If you was a chicken would you lay good with all that racket goin' on?" Then he said a coon must have gotten in and killed them.

I came pretty close to telling him right then and there that if he expected me to swallow a story like that, he must have a brain about the size of a pea. I know what a coon does to a chicken, and it doesn't look anything like that. But I never really said it. I just thought it. And now I'm glad, because all I want is just to see Pa alive, even if he's wrong sometimes.

Momma took her boots off and went into the kitchen and lit the fire in the gas range. She had only got four eggs, and that was just two apiece for Pa and Lemmy, even if me and Momma went without. Pa was yelling about how he was half starved to death, and she couldn't very well expect him to haul an oak limb down off the roof with a half-empty stomach. He told her she'd better fry a whole lot of spuds to make up the difference, and he snapped his suspenders, which Momma hates because it makes them wear out quicker.

Momma was busy with the griddle and slicing some bacon and all, and she said to me without looking, "Ruben, honey, will you go down to the root cellar and bring up some spuds?"

I just stood there. All of a sudden, it didn't matter how bright the sun was shining or how loud the birds were twittering. It might as well have been pitch dark and rain pouring down in buckets again as far as I was concerned. I was thinking about that slime on the front acre and those two empty chicken skins. And I could see the tuckahoe in my head, all smeary through that window in the glare of the lightning, headed straight for the root cellar.

Momma turned and frowned at me when I made no move for the door. Then the frown melted off into worry lines, and she said, "What's wrong, honey?"

"Momma, please don't make me go. There's something down there," I said. My throat was so dry I could hardly get the words out.

Then Pa jumped up out of his chair and grabbed me by the shirt and shook me. I saw the veins popping up on his big, thick neck, and his face was the color of a ripe tomato. I'd have shut my eyes, but I knew that would just make him madder and I was scared that he'd backhand me or kick me as he sometimes does. Instead, he opened up his mouth so those ragged, yellow teeth of his showed like an animal's against the furry dark of his beard. I could feel his breath tickling my cheeks, hot and sharp from the hard cider he had already drunk that morning. I wished he liked me better. Oh, how I wished it.

"You're a good-for-nothin' little momma's boy," he said, soft, almost a whisper. "There ain't nothin' down in that cellar but a few daddy-longlegs and your own damn boogeymen. Now go get them spuds."

He let go of my shirt and shoved me backwards with his fist, and I stumbled like I always do, my feet being so big and my legs so stringy. I landed flat on the floor and I hurt all over, inside and out. I was crying by then, which added even more to my shame. And I started thinking he was probably right. If I was any kind of a real man, I'd get up on my own two feet and go down there after those spuds, whether I was scared or not.

Lemmy stood up and started laughing and prancing around like a girl. "If it's gonna make you cry and all, honey," he said in a high, fake little voice, "*I'll* go get the dad-blamed spuds."

Then I really got mad, because there aren't very many worse things in the world than to have somebody like Lemmy poking fun at you. I don't think I would have done it if I wasn't so mad and if I hadn't wanted so much to prove that I was no sissy. Anyway, I got up and grabbed the basket and started wading through the mud to the root cellar.

There I was, out in the sun again, blue sky above and trees aglitter with dew, just like any other spring morning. Made me feel like I could face most anything. For a minute or two the world seemed so familiar that I started whistling and enjoying the feel of the cool mud between my toes. Then, about a stone's throw from the cellar door, I came across another patch of slime, the same as we had found by the chicken coop.

I squatted down beside it, nearly deaf from the noise of my heart. This slime seemed fresher than the other, and a smell came up from it like from the mouth of a cave that's too dark to see inside of. I stood up slowly, trying not to breathe too fast. My spine felt like ants were marching up it in a long, thick line. Still, I had it in my mind that a man wouldn't run. A man would stay and face whatever came his way.

That's when I heard the sound. It made me think of bees when they swarm in a tree, a thousand little voices raised together to make a single huge and angry one. I looked at the cellar door and I saw it sort of moving, like there was something big leaning on it, trying to get out all at once. There's a crack between the door and the ground, a couple of inches maybe. And through that crack came a mess of gray, wet-looking tuckahoe, moving fast.

Part of me was still trying to act brave, and it said to me, "Ruben, my boy, you must have eaten something that didn't agree with you, for you are seeing things."

But the rest of me, which was the bigger part, said, "If a fellow can't trust his own eyes, just what can he trust?" That bigger part of me didn't give a hoot about whether I was brave or a man or not. It just believed what I was seeing and hearing. That's when I dropped the basket and hightailed it for the house.

By the time I came through the front door, I couldn't even talk. I just stood there shaking and sweating, with my mouth going open and shut. I was peeing my pants. I could feel it washing the mud off my feet onto Momma's clean floor, and I didn't even care. She let out a little cry. Pa got up and stared at me. I don't know what he saw in my face, but it must have convinced him of something, because I have never seen him look like that before. He was scared, and I know it isn't right, but for just one second I was glad.

Pa grabbed his shotgun from the corner, and he said, "All right, Lemmy. We're gonna go find out what the hell is down there." Then him and Lemmy took off for the root cellar.

Momma got her quilt, and she wrapped me up in it and made me sit down on the bench by the fire. She sat beside me, and rocked me and sang to me like she used to do before I got so big. That's all I wanted, just to bury my face in the good clean smells of Momma and forget there was ever anything else.

We sat like that for a long time, waiting for Pa and Lemmy to come back, watching the sun creep past noon into afternoon and the clouds begin to sweep across the sky again. But Pa and Lemmy never came. And we never heard anything for sure, no roar of the shotgun going off, no terrible screams nor cries for help. Once I fancied I heard a kind of long moan, way off across the straw grass. It could have been the wind, or an owl. But somehow, it made me wonder what we'd do if we had to get away. The only gun in the house besides Pa's 10-gauge was Grampa's Colt pistol, which Pa always kept locked in his trunk. I was pretty sure I could break that lock with a hammer. I was pretty sure I could do a lot of things if it came to saving Momma.

After a time, Momma fell asleep, and I did, too, still thinking about that lock. I was just too bone weary to hold my eyes open anymore. I had a dream, a fine warm dream about fishing down by the river on a summer's day, and when I woke up it took me a minute to remember where I was.

The first thing I noticed was that Momma had left the bench. She was standing beside the front door with a butcher knife in her hands, whispering over and over again, "The Lord helps them that helps themselves. The Lord helps them that helps themselves." All at once, it came to me that there was a funny noise outside, like bees swarming in a tree.

I jumped up, tipping over the bench, and yelled, "Momma! Don't, Momma!"

She turned around, and there was a crazy look in her eyes, like I saw once in the eyes of a neighbor woman who stood in the road and watched her house burn down. Momma's face was all shiny with sweat, and that lock of hair had come loose. Oh, how I wanted to tuck it back and make everything all right. "I won't let it in here, Ruben," she said. "I swear I won't." Before I could get to her, she held up the knife and opened the door.

I stood at the window and screamed. I screamed for a long, long time, even after there was nothing left of Momma but skin and clothes and the butcher knife. No matter how she struck and slashed, the tuckahoe got her anyway. And when it was done, it disappeared under the porch, leaving patches of slime on the wood.

Twilight fell before I came to myself enough to get up and light the lamps. I went in and broke Pa's trunk to pieces with Momma's kitchen hatchet and got out the Colt and figured out how to load it.

I have been waiting for Pa and Lemmy to come and tell me it was just a mean trick. But now the rain has started in again.

SHORE LEAVE BLACKS

I stand in the hatchway, watching the quartermaster hunt through boxes of shore leave blacks. There's a tingle in my spine, the irritating buzz that means the most recent hit of bliss is about to wear off. I remember that tomorrow is the last Sunday of August—the traditional day of the family reunion—and anxiety begins to nibble at my stomach again. In another minute or two, the aching exhaustion of a week's insomnia will return. All I can do is try to ignore it. How I wish I hadn't left my blissbox in my cabin.

"Take it easy, Moffat," the quartermaster says as he gives me the blacks. "Your kid'll be fine. You'll see."

My hands shake as I hold up the strange uniform. It's a matte black coverall with silver piping on the sleeves and collar. The idea is to set us apart in a crowd so people will recognize us as lightbuckers and not just ordinary crazies. It looks like plastic, but it feels too soft and slippery for that. It's all one piece. No zippers, no Velcro. I can't even find any meldseams, the sleekest new style when we left. So this is what they're wearing in San Francisco now.

"Maybe I ought to just forget this, Lucky," I say. "Maybe I should just . . ." In the middle of the sentence, I have to clamp my jaw shut to keep my teeth from chattering.

The quartermaster's smile fades till there's only a little of it left. "Maybe you should just do what? Back out and spend your leave on the orbital station?" He shakes his head, but his voice softens. "I hear you signed on for the next Vega run. That's another fifty years, Annie. Think about it. You're never gonna get a second chance to see him."

Lucky's been a lightbucker for two and a half years—six months or a lifetime longer than me, depending on how you look at it. He knows what he's talking about. If I'm ever going to make peace with myself, I must do it now, before my son dies of old age. I squeeze my eyes shut. When I open them again, purple stars float across the shiny alloy of the ship's bulkheads.

Lucky touches my shoulder with a cool, firm hand. "Don't worry so much. You'll be O.K.," he says.

I can't reply. I'm too tired, too afraid that if I speak I'll lose my last shreds of composure. The urge for another hit of bliss has become a maddening itch in my brain.

I nod and try to smile. After a moment, I wad up the blacks, tuck them under my arm, and start down the passageway toward my cabin.

Behind me Lucky calls, "Attagirl."

Lightbuckers always stick together.

Alone in the crew cubicle, I scrabble in my footlocker till I find my blissbox—a lovely thing, intricately inlaid with Eridani gems. I remember the first moment I saw it, in the hands of a bucker named Forrest, in a desert town called Pactolus, a time and place at once beloved and lost. Beside the box lies a snapshot, cracked and dog-eared with handling: the blue sky, the sagebrush plain, the adobe ranch house at the base of the mountains where I grew up.

In the foreground stands a middle-aged woman, smiling, her tan face just beginning to show the effects of a life in the desert sun. Ah, Eugenia Miller, it's easy to imagine you as my mother, perhaps because I knew you better than my real one, who died when I was a child. It's hard to think of you as what you were—the lower-grade teacher in the two-room school where I learned to read.

In the picture, Eugenia holds my baby, Adam, swaddled in a faded patchwork quilt. The infant's face is hidden. All that shows is the top of his silky head. I cannot look at this picture without thinking of my father and my brother, Tim, who haunt it like sullen ghosts. They refused to be in it. Angry because I joined the Light Corps, angry because I came home from my first mission pregnant, angry because I chose to go again and leave them to rear my child. Angrier still at Eugenia Miller because they believed she started it all.

Part of me insists it's only been a year since she posed for this snapshot; Adam must be taking his first few tottery steps by now. But another part of me knows that's a lie. For every minute of my life, almost an hour of theirs has gone by. My father is long since dead; Eugenia and Tim are old, or dead themselves. And Adam? For the barest instant I wonder if, when he reached the age of thirty, he looked anything like Forrest.

I take a blissrock from the box, break it open, and inhale till it hurts.

I emerge from the gleaming orbital shuttle into a world so foreign that I have no idea whether it is better or worse than the one I left. The San Francisco Superterm is a squat, maze-like growth of gray cinder block. Like all such terminals, it stinks of stale food and human sweat. There the familiarity ends. Greenish lights flicker in the darker corners. There are rows of small windows. Through them I glimpse a surreal landscape of hills crowded with windmills, dilapidated shacks, needle-clean office towers, and everything in between.

The windmills have come a long way since I left. They bear little resemblance to the battered steel one that groaned in the dry breeze above my father's ranch. These are gigantic—ten or fifteen meters tall, with long parabolic blades and what must be supercool bearings. They turn though there seems to be no wind at all. I wipe sweat from my forehead. Clearly they don't produce enough electricity for luxuries like air conditioning. I think of the cargo of nuclear fuels we have just brought back from Fomalhaut.

The Light Corps was to have been the lifeline for this energy-hungry world. But looking at these bleak surroundings, I wonder how much difference we have really made.

In the briefing course, they told us all about ground-slicks, the frictionless magnetic trains that are now the most common form of transportation on Earth. But after fifteen minutes of trying to find a ground-slick schedule, I wonder if they made it all up. Outlandishly accoutered people buzz around me like bees, some hurrying past on clear-cut if mysterious errands, others milling in general confusion. Nobody pays the slightest attention to my inquiries. Maybe I'm being too polite.

Finally I grab the sleeve of an efficient-looking middle-aged man as he rushes by. "Do you know where the ground-slick schedules are posted?" I ask.

He frowns, indicates a tiny keyboard on the back of his hand, and says, "Get yourself a wristnet," then hurries on.

I stand there blinking and feeling stupid for a moment. The briefers told us there had been changes in the language. Mostly vocabulary, they said, and they went over a list of new words. But "wristnet" was not among them. I tighten my grip on the handle of my small, black duffel and continue wandering. The briefers also told us the easiest way to deal with time dislocation is to think of Earth as just another alien planet. At the time, I laughed aloud. Now I wish I could take their advice. My powers of self-deception are notoriously good, but even in this stinking terminal I have a terrible case of déjà vu and I can't make myself believe the lie. Earth is not just another alien planet. It's my home. And the people at the end of my journey are not just simple strangers. Once upon a time, they trusted me, and I deserted them.

I sneak into a corner and break open another blissrock, glancing over my shoulder to make sure no one is watching. The briefers were careful to warn us about the various penalties for consumption of illegal substances Earthside. No one approves of blissbreathing; yet everybody does it. Especially lightbuckers.

Eventually, I spy a set of small, deserted LCD screens with a list of ground-slick departures flashing across them in chartreuse letters. The next southbound slick leaves in an hour.

I find a bench and rest on the edge of it for a minute or two, rubbing my thumb across the inlays of the Eridani bliss-box in my hip pocket. I take out the photograph and hold it in my hands like a talisman. I study Eugenia's face. If Adam is still alive, he probably left the ranch long ago. Perhaps the adobe house has fallen to dust. Perhaps there is no one left who cares what I've done, or who remembers that we used to have family reunions on the last Sunday of each August. The thought at once encourages and saddens me.

With a shiver, I get up to look for a ticket window. It takes less time to find than the schedule did. While I wait in line, a teenage girl with a small blue trapezoid painted on her forehead watches me curiously. At first I wonder why. Then I remember the shore leave blacks.

After a while, she says, "Lightbucker, huh? How old are you?"

"Twenty-five," I say.

"No. I mean in real actualness," she says. She sticks something long and purple into her mouth and chews it loudly. It smells like garlic and artificial fruit.

"I'm really twenty-five." I stifle an urge to pull the smelly thing out of her mouth and throw it on the floor. The briefers tried to prepare us for as many changes in customs and styles as they could. But I can already see it was an impossible task.

"No. I mean what is the truest longness of time since you were born?" she says, smacking her lips.

I wrap my fingers around the blissbox in my pocket. I should be a good sport, laugh and tell her exactly what she wants to hear—that I was born eighty years ago, when people still hoped the Light Corps might turn things around for Earth, a long time before blue forehead trapezoids and purple garlic confections came into vogue. But I can't seem to manage it.

"Twenty-five years," I repeat with a broad, stiff grin and turn to the ticket agent.

I hand him my bioprotein card—a small, flat piece of transparent material which contains every bit of information known about me, or so the briefer said. The agent slips it into a slot in the counter, and when it pops out again, he hands it back to me.

"Where's my ticket?" I say.

"You're holding it," he replies. "Next." And he beckons to the girl with the blue trapezoid.

"Uh . . . wait a minute. Where can I buy a newspaper?" It slips out before I remember how foolish it will sound.

He steps back and squints at me. I watch his face change as my blacks register. "Peeeeesuz!" he says; it's almost a whistle. "Maddleford, come here. Alwaysful wanting to see a lightbucker . . ."

Maddleford is a man in his forties whose hair stands up like the fur on an angry dog's back. He has on a jacket that looks like it's made of gold spider webs.

"Newspaper?" says the ticket agent. He is practically screaming with laughter.

"See this?" says Maddleford, pointing to my card. "Take your biopro to an infodist and have it codified in the news slot. Then all you need to do is beam it on your reader."

I stand there for a moment before I realize my mouth is hanging open.

"I'm next, light*fucker*," says the girl with the blue trapezoid. She joins the ticket agent, who is laughing even louder now.

"Shuddup," says Maddleford.

I grab my duffel bag and walk across the depot, holding my chin as high as I can, wishing I could do something about my cheeks, which burn, and my hands, which shake as if I were truly ancient. Before long, I am running as fast as I can down the corridor toward the southbound ground-slick gate.

I pause only a moment on the platform to wipe sweat from my eyes and try to regain my composure. Then I duck through one of the slick's dented aluminum doors and find a seat beside a grimy window. I close my eyes, trying to appear cool and detached. I want to be the tough light-bucker on leave from the stars. I want to be the lean figure on the Saturday vidflicks Tim and I used to watch. But in the darkness behind my eyelids Adam appears. My son, twenty-two years older than I am, abandoned by a mother who wandered off in search of more compelling loves. I lurch forward in my seat, breathing fast, staring at nothing.

From the row in front of mine a little boy gazes at me with his mouth open. He is clutching a stuffed replica of a Centauran silk-spinner.

"Look, Mommy. A lightbucker!" His eyes are big, his voice shrill.

In a sudden fit of shyness, he ducks. Peering at me from between the seat backs, he waves the stuffed spinner over his head. "Sssst ssssst," he says. "I bet you've never seen one of these."

I smile, thinking of Adam. Was he ever like this? "Oh yes, I've seen one of those," I say. "On Alpha Two. The real ones have bigger thoraxes, and they smell like a combination of skunks and rotten eggs."

"Really?" His wide-eyed face reappears above the seats, but only for a moment. I hear the sharp slap of flesh on flesh. "Ow!" he cries.

Then a woman, probably his mother, whispers, "Stop that. It's whippy. Lightbuckers are all brainbent. I don't want you talking to her again."

I am left gazing at the empty seat backs, bitterness rising in the back of my throat. Brainbent. *Freely I give myself to the stars.* That is the oath of the lightbucker. *Freely I afflict myself with the stigmata of temporal physics. Freely I lay down my humanness in return for the beauty of space.* Don't make me laugh.

I run my fingers over the hip pocket of my blacks and the blissbox riding snugly there. I remember my first whiff of bliss, lying in Forrest's arms, looking up at the desert stars of my home as if I had never seen them before. I am infinitely strong, I thought. And all the anger I felt at my circumstances—the death of my mother, the thankless toil of holding a job, keeping house for Father and Tim, and helping with the ranch—was replaced with soft melancholy. I understand, I thought. Finally I understand.

Illusory or not, it's a difficult state of mind to resist. I slip the box from my pocket, break open a rock, and inhale its contents.

Almost immediately I hear polite words from the aisle. "Sorry to bother you, but . . ."

The voice belongs to an immaculate attendant whose clothing, I suspect, is the same color the ground-slick's seat upholstery was before it wore out. He's younger than I am, barely out of his teens, but he places his hand on my shoulder like a favorite uncle giving wise advice. "Buckerfriend, bliss-breathing is antilawful here. Didn't they tell you?"

I regard him for a moment, hoping I will discover something useful about him from his face, his hands, the way he carries himself. I wonder what he will do to me. "Sorry. I didn't know. I won't use any more of them." The lie slips out smoothly.

He smiles in a cordial, practiced way. "Thanks, bucker-friend. But same in same, I have to take them away."

All I can think of is the prospect of facing Adam with-out the help of bliss. I have a few extra rocks hidden in my duffel, but I'm not sure they'll be enough to get me through. A tingle of panic buzzes upward from my groin. I feel the muscles in the back of my neck tighten. "What do you mean? They're mine."

"It's antilawful to possess them. Sorry," he says.

"Look. Just let me keep them. I'm not bothering any-one."

He turns and beckons to someone I can't see. A larger attendant hurries down the aisle.

"Please don't," I say, in as quiet a voice as I can manage. They pay no attention. The new arrival pries my fingers open and takes away the Eridani blissbox. I watch him touch it, hating him, feeling as if he were violating my own body. The other passengers whisper behind their hands.

"The box isn't yours. At least let me keep the box," I say.

He opens it, shakes the blissrocks into the palm of his hand, and pockets them. Smirking, he tosses the box to the first attendant, turns, and walks back the way he came. I pound the armrests softly with my palms, cursing the guilt that made me embark on this journey, wishing for the familiar comfort of unexplored planets.

But a second later, I feel the initial tendrils of euphoria wrap around me as that last, expensive hit of bliss finally begins to take effect.

I notice that the first attendant's cheeks are red. An apologetic smile jerks across his face and disappears as he hands the empty box back to me. I'm fascinated by his teeth, which are horribly white. Briefly, I hope I have ruined his day. Then the main rush of bliss floods through me, the ground-slick shudders out of the station, and I realize my anger is not worth the energy it takes to sustain it.

I close my eyes, enjoying the way a smile feels on my face. Of course everything will be fine. I picture myself scuffling through the dusty remains of the adobe ranch house. Nobody will be there. Least of all Adam. It hardly matters anyway.

I imagine the earth without people. It would all be so much easier then. Sky. Continents. Mountains. Rocks. Maybe these are the things I have really come back for. Entities that change at a meaningful rate—not at all in a hundred human life spans. But in fact my mind is on people. Tim, my father, Adam, and especially Eugenia Miller, who was kind to me when no one else chose to be. I loved a lightbucker once. He said he would take me to the stars and grow old with me. I believed him. Exhausted, I doze.

I dream of Forrest.

On a warm, windy night he comes to the café where I work. We can see the stars through the dust, and he points out the ones he has been to. Over coffee, he watches me with his flame-blue eyes and tells me the story of his life. When I bring him his check, he lays the Eridani blissbox on the tray. I have never seen anything like it before. "Keep it," he says. "Let me take you somewhere. I have no one. No one in all the world except you." I imagine his home, a town in the north—the snow, the heavy gray sky, the streets filled with strangers. "Dead, or transformed by time, all of them," he says.

I hold the blissbox in the palm of my hand. It feels warm, as if it contains all the fire of the stars. The heat goes up my arm, down my spine in a shiver of longing, and I know nothing will ever be the same again.

I struggle to stay in the warmth of this moment, but the dream fades into an old, familiar one. I am standing on the ramp of a Lux drive starship waiting for Forrest. I have just returned from the leave I took to bear our son; this ship is bound for Fomalhaut, and Forrest and I have both signed on for the run. I was to meet him here.

Instead, it's a cosmocop who meets me. Sadness clings to him like dust. I see it in the soft lines of his face, even on his boots and dark uniform. He holds something out to me. A padded envelope bearing the official insignia of the Light Corps.

"I'm terribly sorry," he says. "The ensign was a good man. I knew him personally."

I stare down at the envelope, knowing what's in it. A stilted letter about a loading accident on an asteroid. For a moment, I can't breathe. Then the dream disappears, and there's nothing left. Nothing left at all except blackness.

When I awaken, we have already come far south, stopping at small places along the way no doubt, and are hurtling through the mountains. In a few minutes, we will reach Pactolus. I stare out the window, lost in a game of pretend. I'm sixteen years old. I'm riding in an automobile, and beside me sit Tim and my father. We're on our way home to the Lost Cannon Ranch. I know these meadows, these granite cliffs. They will look the same forever. The stars are only a dream. There is no Adam. And relativity is an esoteric mind game played for amusement by certain academics.

The fantasy abruptly disintegrates as the little boy I spoke to earlier begins to wail for unknown reasons.

The question returns: What will I say to my son?

The slick stops only a few seconds in Pactolus. I step onto the platform, the strap of my duffel bag twisted around my wrist so tightly it almost cuts off the circulation. There's a slight rush of cool air as the train pulls away. Then I am alone.

The Lost Cannon Ranch lies four miles from here, at the end of a dirt road. More precisely, if the Lost Cannon Ranch still exists, it lies four miles from here, and the road was dirt forty-seven years ago.

I walk toward the tiny station house. The sun pours down from a fierce blue sky, baking everything—the wood, the rocks, the sagebrush, and especially me, in my imprac-tical black uniform. Somehow, I had forgotten the magnitude of this dry heat. I loosen my collar.

Inside the station, there's an office with a counter and a window. A sign above it says Tickets and Information. The person inside does not look up when I speak.

"I want to go out to the Lost Cannon. What's the best way to get there?" I say, and then hold my breath.

"Go down to Naylor's and rent a sandscoot."

I start to breathe again, a little shakily. He recognizes the name. The ranch must still be there.

"What's a sandscoot?"

Now he raises his head, frowning. I'm relieved to discover that he is a mere baby, a boy in his early twenties, far too young to be anyone I know.

"Waddya mean, what's a sandscoot?" he says. His speech patterns seem more familiar, less modern, than those I heard in the superterm. At least one thing remains unchanged. The mainstream of progress still takes a long time to touch a place as small as Pactolus.

I stand in fidgety silence while he looks at me. I would like nothing better than to abandon this exchange and find a secluded place to do a blissrock.

His expression goes from suspicion to excitement as he realizes I'm dressed in a bucker's uniform. "Peesuz, you must be Annie Moffat!"

"That's right," I say as he shakes my hand across the counter. "How did you know my name?"

"Old Tim said to stay sharp for lightbuckers, because you might show for the reunion this year. They keep track of the ships. You're famous around here, did you know that?" he says.

"No." Old Tim. Still alive. In a single sentence, the boy behind the counter has blasted away the possibility that nothing will happen. There will be no dusty ruins. The family will gather. And the last Sunday of August looms in my future as surely as tomorrow's sunrise. I struggle to control the panic that rises inside me. I don't want to be famous. I don't want Tim to be keeping track of the ships. I wish everyone had forgotten about me.

The counter boy continues with horrible good cheer. "My name's Jerry Blue. Pleased to meet you." He flashes me a big, easy grin. "My granddad says you went to school with him."

Blue. I think I remember this alleged grandfather. A kid with big ears who had a black dog named Sandy. The storm of panic abates a little, and with it the itch for a blissrock. I return the boy's smile in spite of myself. I take a deep breath.

"Tell me. What's a sandscoot?" I say.

"Well, it's . . . peesuz, haven't you ever seen a sand-scoot?"

I shake my head again and lick salty sweat from my upper lip.

"Naw, now that I think of it. Sandscoots have only been around since '70. Peesuz. You've been gone a long time."

Oh no, I want to say. You just *think* I've been gone a long time. You're crazy. It's only been a year. "Sandscoot," says Jerry Blue. "It's a single-passenger wheel for rough terrain hopping." He wrinkles his forehead. "I just thought of something, though. You got a VO permit?"

"I don't know. Maybe," I say. I hand him my biopro.

"Two secs real time. I'll find out." He slides the card into the omnipresent slot in the counter and drums his fingers while he waits for information to appear on an LCD screen. "Sorry," he says. "I'm saving up for a wristnet, but I don't have it yet." He taps the back of his hand like the man in the superterm who also talked of wristnets.

My puzzlement must show, for he adds, as the LCD begins to glow with text, "You know about wristnets? It's kind of . . . peesuz . . . hard to explain. Like having a computer link straight to your brain. It's faster."

I try, without much success, to imagine what it would be like to have a computer link straight to my brain.

Jerry Blue glances at the screen, hands the card back to me. "No vehicle operator's permit. I didn't think so. Naylor can't rent you a sandscoot without one."

A new obstacle. From the beginning, this journey has been like trying to map a type-four planet. Maybe all these problems are fate's way of telling me I shouldn't be doing this. God, I need a blissrock. I fight the impulse to fling myself through the doorway and run northward along the ground-slick tracks until this place is invisible, not even a smudge on the horizon. I know it won't work. Wherever I go, I carry Pactolus and the Lost Cannon and all their inhabitants inside me. The only way to escape is to face them.

Jerry Blue leans an elbow on the counter and scratches his head. "Say. Do you know how to ride a horse?"

Here at last is something I can understand. We look at each other, and both of us smile at the same time.

He locks up the station, and we walk down the main street of town. It's been paved since I saw it last, though the asphalt is full of potholes now. Two gigantic windmills rise in the distance like trees transplanted from some alien ecosystem. But the air smells familiar. Sagebrush and dust.

We pass the post office with its flagpole, and the patch of lawn where I turned my first somersault. There is Oxoby's Mercantile. Someone painted it pink—about ten years ago, judging from its condition. But the entrance stands open, and I recognize the old ceiling fan that stirs the air in the dark interior of the store. There is the Majestic Theater, boarded up now. And the school. And Joe and Lila's, where I waited tables and met a bucker named Forrest. It has a new name. Porky's Cafe. They've replaced the old leather booths with plastic tables and chairs. The sight leaves me suddenly empty.

I fidget with the meldseams of my duffel. I could reach into it as we walk. Refill the Eridani blissbox with rocks. Nobody in this hick town would even know what I was doing.

"We'll ask Eugenia Miller if you can use one of her horses," says Jerry Blue. "Maybe you know her. She used to teach school."

The name jolts me out of my daydream. "Who did you say?"

"Eugenia Miller."

We have stopped at the south end of the street. To our right stands a white Victorian, the first building I have seen since my arrival that looks as if someone cares about it. Behind the house stretches a fenced field, kept green by a tiny irrigation ditch. Two horses graze at its banks, snorting and stamping in the heat. I know this place. Its owner taught me many things—among them that the world extends beyond Pactolus.

Eugenia was young then, a schoolmarm widow who lived in this wooden house with her small daughter, Rose. I envied the child. Rosie had no father to torment her for lacking the strength of a son, no older brother to live up to. And she had what I would have given in exchange for life itself: a mother.

I slip my hand into my pocket and run my fingertips across the cracked finish of the photograph, now moist with sweat, the picture of Eugenia holding my son. "Annie," she used to say, "you're bright. With a little work, that brain of yours will take you wherever you want to go."

A torrent of memories pours down on me like desert rain. How I kicked Billy Harper in the shins so I could stay after school to clean blackboards. How I lingered afternoons at this whitewashed gate till Eugenia, with a smile and a sigh, appeared on the porch and beckoned me in for milk and cookies. How she single-handedly persuaded my stubborn father to let me go away to college. And how, years later, she rocked my baby in her arms and said, "It's no crime to love more than one thing. Follow your heart, my dear."

I hear the rush of my own blood as a small, wrinkled woman in jeans and boots answers Jerry Blue's knock. How old would she be? I figure a sum in my head. Eighty-seven. Eighty-eight. "How are you, Jerald? What brings you out today?" she says, brushing a wayward lock of white hair from her eyes. Perhaps he was once a student of hers. I do another mental sum. No. He's far too young.

"Somebody special needs a horse, Eugenia, and I thought you might be willing to lend one of yours," says Jerry Blue. He gestures at me, standing behind him in the cool shade of the porch. "It's one of these lightbucker Moffats, here for the big reunion. Old Tim's sister."

Something about the wording of that statement seems odd, but I have no more than a second or two to wonder about it before the thought is lost to more important ones. For Eugenia is peering at me, her green eyes as bright and intense as marbles set in the unfamiliar wrinkles of her flesh.

"My God, Annie," she murmurs. "They said you'd live forever, and it must be true. You don't look a day older. Not one day." The bright eyes fill with tears. She rises on tiptoes to enfold me in her arms. At last, I can cry, too.

The horse is Eugenia's favorite, a glossy black gelding called Night Sky. With strength belying her age, she throws a black Spanish saddle tooled with silver over his back. I protest. "It's too valuable! It might be stolen."

She laughs. "In Pactolus? Come to your senses, girl. Climb up there, and not another word about it. The saddle doesn't get used half as often as it should since Rosie left home. Why, you in your black outfit, and Night Sky in his, all decked with silver, the two of you will look like you rode right down from the stars." She winks at me. "Besides. A grand entrance is always good for the soul."

I smile, mount, lean over the stirrup to kiss her, wondering how much she knows about what's waiting for me. The panic swirls up again, and I have to spend a long moment, eyes closed, steadying myself.

Eugenia reaches up and squeezes my hand. "If it's any comfort to you," she says, "every woman's child grows up to be a stranger." She shakes her head and looks away across the desert. "I guess almost anything can make a mother feel guilty."

She looks back at me with a quick smile, then slaps the horse on the rump and cries, "Giddyup! They're waiting for you."

Night Sky is a good horse—spirited but responsive. Black, I think, as he takes me over the road. Black for space. Black for the bucker. Black for the absence of light. Four miles isn't far for such a fine animal. I don't urge him. Instead, I let him set his own pace, except for the moments when my courage fails me. Then I pull gently on the reins and hold him prancing among the sagebrush and junipers. Three times I stop and reach for my duffel bag. Twice I leave it unopened. The third time I hold a blissrock in my shaking hand and stare at it, finally returning it unbroken to the bag. *No more,* I think. *For this, I must be myself.*

Long before we reach the ranch, the sun fattens, almost touching the hills. The horse's hooves stir the dust of the desert, make it shimmer in the oblique rays of evening. I make him dance in circles while I try to steel myself yet again for what lies ahead. We move on awhile. Then I stop him again, and we move on again. In this way, we come at last to the gate of the Lost Cannon.

The house is still there, already lying deep in the shadow of the mountains. One of the tall poplar trees has disappeared. The windmill has been replaced with a newer model. The porch sags a little. Figures move in its dim shelter. In the still, dry air, crickets have begun to sing. Quiet voices carry from the porch, a sound so vividly familiar that for a moment it makes me dizzy. On this, the night before the last Sunday of August, the gathering has already begun.

Night Sky whickers as someone approaches through the blue twilight, holding up an electric lantern. "Hello. Who's there?" It's a man's voice.

"Annie. Annie the lightbucker." This is the moment. The moment when I push away from the hull of the ship, trusting my life to a frail rope of human manufacture.

I dismount from the horse, patting his neck, willing myself to hold the reins loosely as if I were calm and relaxed. The man's pace quickens. He stops a few yards from me. The dusk is so deep that I still can't make out his face. In my pocket, my hand is a fist around Forrest's empty Eridani blissbox.

"Annie? Your name is Annie?" says the voice in the darkness.

"Yes," I say. "The one who's been away a long time. The one who . . ."

"I know," he says. "They say you left your child behind because you loved space and lightbuckers more. My mother. You're my mother."

The breath rushes out of me. For a moment, I can make no sound at all. Then, "I . . . Adam, I . . . *I'm so sorry.*" I don't even know if my words are intelligible. I seem dissolved in tears. I hear them, pat, pat, falling into the dust at my feet. I want to stop, but it's useless. The pain is too great. I scrub my sleeve across my eyes, trying to replace the pain with disgust at my own behavior. Anything is better.

Adam draws nearer. I can almost smell him—a clean, moist scent like the vigorous breath of a child. In a moment, I see him more clearly through the gloom, and a second shock hits me.

How old must he be? Forty-seven. Forty-seven. I have long since memorized it. But I can see him well enough to be certain of one thing. This Adam is young. Twenty-two. Twenty-three. Even younger than I am.

"It's all right. I'm glad you came. Mother." The last word comes slowly, as if he's trying it out, listening to the sound of it. I hear the scrape of his boots as he scuffs them against the ground. "I wanted to tell you that I understand. I do. I understand."

He holds the lantern higher, and for the first time since his infancy, I see him in completeness. I step toward him, the ache inside me fluttering now, like a bird considering flight. His suit looks like plastic, but it's too soft. It's all one piece, and it has no zippers, no Velcro, not even any meld-seams. He is wearing shore leave blacks.

His laughter is bright and pure as the light of suns. Oh yes, he understands, and I laugh along with him, relishing the sound of it. He links his arm through mine.

Above us, the first stars appear.